Sad and Angry Man

(52,000 words)

by Phillip Good

To purchase more fine books like the one you're reading, go to http://zanybooks.com.

Chapter 1

I let myself go, I reach down toward the sadness.

I'm not sure my father ever really loved me. He took me places he wanted to go, football games (never hockey, I liked hockey), baseball (I saw Jackie Robinson break into the big leagues), and the golf course (he taught me to swing left-handed, his way, and ever since I've thrown right and batted left).

Later, in my teens, when I didn't do what he wanted, he cut me off completely. He didn't speak to me or try to contact me after my sixteenth year, not even a letter.

It took me so long to learn to love my mother. I dumped all the hatred and anger on her that I felt toward my father.

She collapsed once on the steps of the bus that was taking us to Nova Scotia on a vacation she could ill afford. I pretended I did not see her fall; my younger brother was not conscious of what had happened; the other passengers and the driver rushed to her aid; "Anemia," she said after she'd been attended to.

I ran away from home, failed at it, and came running back to her again and again.

I have always been an angry person. There is no injustice over which I'm unwilling to rage. The daily paper sends me into a frenzy—corrupt politicians, libraries with $5 million for construction and nothing for books, pro-lifers who kill. But I cry, too, over a story of a small child kidnapped from his parents, and the photograph of another child, a victim of a bombing, viewed standing outside the remnants of her burned-out home. If I were God . . . But I am not. I don't have the power to set things right. I can only stand, my blood pressure rising, and rage.

Many people use their sadness to mask a harsh aggressive anger; I am just the other way around. When I started working with Dr Berman, my new therapist, he taught me to go beneath my anger, to tap the well of sadness that my anger camouflages.

Bring back that time of sadness now. Bring back those days of weeping, the three months in therapy with Dr Berman, the six months afterward.

Dr Berman was not a good person. A masterful technician, perhaps; his therapeutic skills brought me back to his office week after week, two hours on the freeway for each hour of attention, but his narcissism, his lack of consideration for others were why I left.

I learned from him to accept my father's rejection and to forgive myself. I am no longer quick to anger and if I do grow angry, it is an anger I can control, can work with, can shape.

Once while hypnotized—another of Dr Berman's "techniques," I regressed back to my mother's womb, to perhaps six months after my conception. I could hear my mother thinking, or thought I could: "My mother will respect me now." she thought.

So I know why I am the way I am, compulsive and determined to succeed. I am acting out my mother's fantasy of pleasing her mother. I forgive my mother for her own need to succeed, her own way of going about it. Now that I forgive myself, I can forgive others.

I reach down and touch the sadness.

Dr Berman was trained in psychodrama and is licensed in hypnotherapy. Despite or because of this training, he sees his patients only as a means to an end—money and his own self-gratification.

His narcissism is insufferable. At the end of each session, he has his patients recite a credo. Standing behind me, he whispers in my ear:

"I'm getting better."

"I'M GETTING BETTER," I repeat in a loud voice.

"I'm a good person."

"I'M A GOOD PERSON."

"I can relax now."

"RELAX."

"and let Dr Berman make my decisions for me."

""

The silence hangs in the air between us. Whatever poise I've gained from the hour is gone. I don't know whether Dr Berman is happy or unhappy that I will not recite his credo.

"I'll let Dr Berman make my decisions..." he repeats tentatively, before his voice trails off. But happy/unhappy I might be, I will let no other person make my decisions for me. The imprint of my mother/father/grandmother/grandfather is too strong for that.

Dr Berman's inner corruption was revealed most clearly at our last late-evening group session. I watched him yawn, not even bothering to cover his mouth, while Joan our child-abused child-abuser spilled out her guts to him. And should I forgive you for this act of rudeness, Doc, because you work long hours, sixteen a day, at $150 per?

Dr Berman insists on being paid at the end of each session.

"My insurance will pay."

"We'd like you to pay up front. When your insurance does come through, we can apply what you've already paid to your future co-payments."

We could, I suppose, if I planned to spend the rest of my life on the freeway driving to your office twice a week. But I came here to be cured, today, now.

"You are hostile," Dr Berman says, "reach down for the sadness."

I am a sad and angry man. I reach inside and we part angrily.

He telephoned me several times afterwards. "The other members of the group miss you," he said.

"And I miss them too," I replied, sobbing, for I felt in fleeing him I had abandoned them.

The crying continued for more than six months afterward. I cried for my lost children, my lost life, my father ridiculed by his father, ridiculing his sons in turn, and my mother, ridiculed and belittled first by her mother, then her husband, and then her sons. I cried for what I could have been and for what I have become. I am a sad and angry man.

The crying stopped; the sadness never left me.

I turn to the newspaper: "When Huldi was twelve years old, the police, responding to allegations of child abuse, came to her fifth-grade classroom and took her away. Afterward, she was shuttled from one foster-care home to another, thirteen in six years, to be discharged from the system six years later without a high school diploma."

I continue reading. "Huldi's first nights on the street were spent in an alleyway. Over the course of the next few weeks, she met other abandoned teenagers. Two months ago, she and six of her friends stumbled upon a condemned apartment building that had been damaged in a fire. They live there together now."

Huldi's best friend was raped last week. She told the reporter she hoped she and the other teenagers could stay together as a family; "we hold each another when one of us has a bad dream; we steal enough each day to live."

Sitting over a second cup of coffee, reading this story, I burst into tears. Yet other people, normal people whom I might meet and marry, could have the girl herself, dirt-stained and weeping, walk up to their cars to beg for money, and not feel a thing.

"Just before her 18th birthday, Huldi was handed a token for her bus fare and a Hefty garbage bag to hold her belongings and was told the government was no longer responsible for her." I read and I burst into tears.

Chapter 2.

My life may be divided into five distinct periods, perhaps six:

A time of innocence—what do they call this period now, the wonder years?—when one just grows and learns by observation. I lived my life free of introspection and dwelt in the here and now.

A time to study—in my case, a rather prolonged period, for I had a double major in college, went on to graduate school, and took forever to get my doctorate. I had fun though, in a strange way. I liked learning, liked to bury my nose in a book, and if I lusted after girls more often than I slept with them, still each small gain, a kiss, a hand on a breast, burned in my memory.

A time of stupidity, when, in my first two or three jobs, I gave no thought to the future, prepared no cover-your-ass memos, and changed jobs on a whim, once, simply because I had broken up with a girlfriend. Like a grasshopper, I stored nothing away, and, worse, I left a trail of burned bridges that would soon need to be crossed.

The time of marriage—the flood tide of which Shakespeare writes in Henry V, leading on to victory. I know I accomplished a number of important things during this period. I wrote and published articles, a book ("Inside the Human Cell"), solved problems (I was part of the study team that developed Motrin, a.k.a. Ibuprofen and Advil), and had three joy-providing daughters whom I followed from diapers to soccer uniforms.

We lived during this period in a rural area outside of Kalamazoo instead of in urban West Los Angeles but, you know, I don't think I noticed the difference. My life was much as it had been in my time of innocence. I did too much each day for it to really matter where I was: attending Lamaze classes, giving late night feedings, taking off from work in midday to attend elementary-school pageants and middle-school track meets, ferrying kids to and from soccer games (three kids could mean three fields on a single day), hosting slumber parties, chaperoning dances.

Once my retirement was vested, I stopped working for someone else and went into business with my wife as a partner. (Hence, the possibility of dividing the time of my marriage into two periods, one as worker bee, a second as entrepreneur). And then, abruptly, I was divorced.

I was also unemployed. My business simply crumbled without someone there to keep me organized and to give me the incentive for carrying on. Ask any self-employed person: the secret to making twice as much money is to work twice as many hours as you would if you worked for somebody else. But my wife and partner had left, taking my two youngest children with her; my oldest would be leaving in six months to go to college; what was the point?

If you want a date with a girl, the first thing you must do is ask her. The several variants to Nancy's rule—(don't ask me to explain or remember who Nancy was; I think I met her at an Alumni Club dance)—include all of the following: if you want a story or a book to be accepted you must first submit it to a publisher; if you want to win a tournament, you've got to show up on the court; and if you want a job, you've got to turn in an application.

I didn't apply. I waited at home for the telephone to ring. An old friend from work will call, I prayed, or a former client, wondering what has become of me.

But of course, no one called or, if they did, it was with troubles of their own.

"Hi, this is Saul. Remember me?"

"From the conference, sure." I lied.

"Looks like Boeing is going to start laying people off. I know you started a business, how is it doing?"

And before I could tell the truth, Saul or Bill, or any of the half-dozen others who called me during the country's latest economic downturn would tell me about the many skills they'd use to solve my problems, to make more money for the two of us.

I would interrupt finally, and tell them how things stood. Always, a slight intake of breath result along with a pause in which I could hear the wheels turning. They would say they were concerned, that two heads were better than one, that they would be on the lookout for a job for me while they were looking for a job for themselves. And I would never hear from them again.

Still, networking is the first step toward getting a new and better job. The self-help books are very clear about this. Whether you've been fired, divorced, or laid-off, you've got to get out and circulate.

Join Toastmasters and three or four professional societies. Volunteer for committees. Why not, you've plenty of time. Build a network and something will turn up.

For others, maybe. The truth is I build friendships slowly. One every six years, perhaps. Someone I meet at work or maybe even someone who just sat next to me on an airplane. We exchange phone calls, have a beer when one or the other of us is in the area, maybe even go out with our wives for a night on the town. So I'm 49 and have five friends. One lives in Australia. Two still need me more than I need them. One died of juvenile-onset diabetes. I didn't even know Jim had diabetes till the very end, when he was on dialysis and the transplant didn't take. "What did you expect," Jim grinned, "that you'd know I was a diabetic because I'd be shooting up [insulin] in the men's room." Bye Jim, I'll miss you. But it was Jim's partner Mark, my ex boss, who called to tell me about the job opportunity.

Chapter 3.

I was born in Montreal, Quebec, which sounds frightfully exotic, and would have been except I was not born French, but one of the several hundred thousand anglaises (English) that would soon be driven from their own country by the cradle's revenge as we termed the burgeoning French population.

I didn't know all this then. I mean I was born, suckled happily, gurgled, responded well to tickling and other external stimuli—"good signs," the doctor said, and had a remarkably happy childhood, up to age six.

Oh, I have a few unhappy memories. "They don't allow Jews in Westmount," I'd heard someone say and I wondered, "What are Jews?"

"We're Jews," my parents told me which didn't clear up much of anything since my parents did not attend synagogue and religion played a negligible role in my early life.

I can still remember the kids stopping me in front of the school one day and telling me I couldn't come in. "Why not?" I asked.

"It's a Jewish holiday," they said pointing to the school calendar where the faint indelible letters j.h. were scattered across the days.

"What holiday are we celebrating?" I asked my mom.

"I don't know," she replied.

Mostly, I was a very happy baby and a very happy child and I still have a photograph in black and gray to prove it. See the kid in the snowsuit with the long scarf wrapped around his neck and face and little more than his eyes showing, that's me. I remember my mother putting the snowsuit on me early in the morning, tying on my skies and leaving me out all winter, or until it was time to come in and eat hot Campbell's soup with crackers and a glass of milk.

When I was seven, my parents divorced. We moved out of the province for a while, back to rural Manitoba where my mother's parents, my grandparents lived. We moved again several times after we returned to Montreal. Moves that were just in time to leave me behind in a different subject at each new school I attended.

At age twelve, I began attending the High School of Montreal, a magnet school located in downtown Montreal across the street from

McGill University, where very tough and very studious kids all mixed. I had some rough times there and I had some great ones. Often both the good and the bad in a single day.

Four years ago, on my forty-fifth birthday, I decided I was ready to go back and confront the kids I'd gone to school with. A man, now, with muscles in the places they are supposed to be, a wife, kids of my own, and a good job—I'd even published a book—I called the school to find out when the next reunion was. Closed. Replaced by the new Francophile government with L'Ecole Technique, a trade school, with all classes taught in French. I haven't been back to Montreal High, or to Montreal, or McGill since.

McGill University provided me with a bachelor's degree and the insight I needed to start learning on my own. McGill is right across the street from the high school. The big difference was that when I went to high school, I lived at home and had to spend an hour or so on streetcars each day. (Sometimes, when the snow blocked the tracks and the trolleys couldn't get through, that hour would be spent walking over Mont Royale, the gently sloped mountain that defines and delineates my beautiful city.) When I went to college, I lived on campus in a dorm, and when I wasn't in class or the library, I was running across the mountain for exercise and in the hopes of making and then staying on the cross-country team.

From McGill, I went to UCBerkeley and another monastic existence, but . . . who cares. What happened was that I didn't go to McGill Medical School, a serious mistake, economically. Instead, I got a Ph.D. and the training I needed to be a professor.

My first teaching job, fresh out of Berkeley, was not a success. Somewhere along the line, my mother had converted from Judaism to a small fundamentalist Christian sect. In my father's absence, we were strapped for cash, and I made it through college only with the aid of a series of small grants from her church. Feeling an obligation to repay them, I turned aside offers from my advisors to obtain positions for me at Nebraska and Vanderbilt, and rejected outright an offer from the University of Chicago that I somehow obtained on my own. I traveled instead to Flagstaff Arizona and a tiny liberal-arts college run by the Brethren of Christ. There, I rented a cabin in the nearby Ponderosa forest—the rent was nominal, the view of the tall pines and Douglas firs spectacular—and settled in for a year of "service."

My undoing was a stack of Playboys. Just as Gideon left his Bible for the comfort of the weary traveler, the former occupant of the cabin left his Playboys to comfort and show me the way. I'd been suppressing my natural urges for years at the behest of my monkish academic superiors: "Study. Study. Marriage will come later." Those magazines put me over the top.

Not that I did anything outrageous; I didn't make passes at my students or anything like that. But my conversation and my lectures began to be spiced with the sort of double entendres that are characteristic of Playboy, especially in the two-page section of humor that follows the centerfold. These sexual allusions put my students on guard; some actually reported me for my "jokes," though nothing was done about it at the time.

A party I hosted was the climax. My guests were my students—most of my fellow faculty members were married and didn't particularly care for me. Alcohol was consumed and some born-again Christians broke into my bedroom and discovered walls lined with Playmates-of-the-Month. The next day, half a dozen of my "guests" reported me to the school authorities. (How they managed to do this without betraying themselves remains a mystery; I suppose they might have been allowed to copy out a hundred Bible verses by way of penance.)

The authorities investigated; I wasn't fired immediately, but all the female students were removed from my classes and interrogated one by one. A very thick dossier confronted me on the Vice-President's desk when I was finally summoned for an interview.

I was shocked, wounded as much or more by the students' betrayal as by the prospect of losing my job. I hadn't been much good with people before—think of me as a ten-year old, content to have playmates come and go, not mean-spirited, but insensitive. Now, I knew that people were something to be feared. Humiliated, hearing the Vice-President's voice as something distant and unconnected with me, I began to build a shell around me to isolate and shield me from others. And though the Vice-President's words failed to reach my head—where intellect still reined supreme—they penetrated deep in my gut, leaving me devoid of all self-confidence.

My firing was not completely without its rewards. Learning that I'd been "permitted" to stay on until the end of the term, three young ladies, curious about the ways of the world, called upon me, the campus' only known roué, to instruct them. If my knowledge were less than theirs, they overlooked this deficit, and certainly by the end of my days at Flagstaff, Playboys were no longer necessary as a stimulus for my imagination.

Wow, that was a long time ago, years and years and years. This is supposed to be a resume of a sad and angry man's life, not his whole life story. O.K., I made mistakes, was or felt betrayed, grew older and more experienced, began to hide the real Peter Wood under a facade of bullshit and bravado. Suppose we switch now, quickly, to resume form:

> Received B.A. from McGill and Ph.D. from the University of California at Berkeley. (Advisors: DeOhm and Nandi).
>
> Assistant Professor, Flagstaff College, Flagstaff AZ.
>
> Postdoctoral fellowship at the University of Pennsylvania (an attempt by one of my advisors to rehabilitate me).
>
> Five years with Upjohn Pharmaceutical in Kalamazoo MI trying to clone lung cells that would thrive on smog. The work I did for Upjohn on Rogaine/Regain during its early stages, when it was still under consideration as a blood-pressure regulator, endeared me to Upjohn's administrators. Had I hung around, I might have become rich on the profits generated when Rogaine/Regaine became a cure for baldness. As it was, I left Upjohn to pursue an entrepreneurial opportunity.
>
> Operations Manager, Information Research, Mattawan MI, a firm specializing in laboratory integration and direct data acquisition.

And what happened to Information Research? Well, you might as well ask what happened to my marriage. Information Research was us. When there was no more us, there was no more company. The loss of the woman I loved, and had thought loved me, brought my business to a halt, drained my spirit—though it left my brash and acerbic personality—and took away the last of my confidence. The economy, too, was in recession, and, suddenly, no more jobs were to be had, anywhere.

Problem: You have three children, one is in college, and two are headed in that direction; you have no job, no marriage and no immediate prospects. Suddenly, out of the blue, as the result of the efforts of a friend you didn't know you had, you receive a job offer from an obscure college in the backwoods of a southern state your abolitionist soul deplores. Do you take this job or do you let your kids drop out of school and sign up full time as waitresses at Chuckie Cheese?

"After all," I told my friends, "I'm just going to Georgia for an interview."

"After all," I told my daughters after Benjamin, a traditionally black college located an hour and a half from Atlanta in central Georgia, made me an offer, "I'll just be there for three years, long enough to see you all through school. We'll get together on vacations. You guys will be in class the rest of the time, so you'll barely notice the difference."

Maybe my kids bought this explanation, maybe they didn't. I conned myself, anyway.

Chapter 4

Five days and two thousand miles after my departure from my home in Michigan, I exited the Interstate, parked briefly, and referred one more time to the detailed map with which I'd been supplied.

Fort Lee, where Benjamin College is located, is deep in the hinterland, an hour and a half south of Atlanta. As the map became a reality, I became increasingly nervous. I'm not unaccustomed to greenery, at decent intervals, nor to banked and graded turns. But here, one farm blended into the next, interrupted perhaps by a cemetery, a trailer park, a combination Bar B-Q and filling station; the road bent back upon itself in a hairpin turn only to unwind amid another long level stretch of green.

"Pecans," the signs promised which explained the long rows of tall nut-laden trees and the shack-like holding sheds with the boxes stacked outside.

Just when I thought I was adjusted to farm and forest, no longer needing a Stones tape to keep me urban and sane, the road reached the outskirts of Fort Lee and an abbreviated downtown with four fried-chicken places on a single corner, a Penny's catalog store, a lawyer's office, and a realtor's; the streets were deserted, the occupants shuttered indoors out of the heat. Small town, USA: I could handle it. But then, unexpectedly, my car came amidst lines of concrete tenements and a scene straight out of West Africa.

The dusty unpaved road teamed with life. Here walked a negress with a basket of laundry atop her head; close behind, the bandanned head of a second black woman bore a giant box of Tide. The pair was headed for the laundromat, but their free flowing strides might have come out of some National Geographic film.

I passed the doorway of a triplex where three black male figures sat on a stoop, passing a vodka bottle back and forth. Barefoot black children ran in and out of doorways, their white-rimmed eyes never meeting mine.

All the faces that I saw were black, not hostile, but indifferent, disconcerting because they were so disparate from what I was used to. They scared me. At that instant, I only wanted to be somewhere else.

Benjamin is an all-black college, conceived in the thirties as a segregated alternative to whites-only Georgia Tech and the University of Georgia at Athens. State financial support increased dramatically in the fifties, when the fear arose that federal courts might not be sympathetic to a $50,000-for-you, $5-million-for-us approach to black and white education. In the seventies, with all schools in Georgia integrated (in theory, not practice) state support dropped to a minimum. The whites left Benjamin (had any attended to begin with?) and it was once again segregated and all-black.

I'd known this—how could I not know, I'd been to the college for an interview—but I'd set my knowledge of its blackness aside, for I needed the job, desperately.

I have no particular understanding or affinity for black people. I'm a Canadian, born in Quebec. I didn't see my first black person until I was six years old and then only as an accident of history because Montreal, years before the Expos (and Expo '68 itself), housed a Dodgers' farm team.

My father asked me if I'd like to see a black man. I said "yes," as I'd have said yes, then, to anything that promised a trip somewhere with my dad.

The stadium was filled. The black man appeared as promised at second base. He hit a single. And Jackie Robinson, the Brooklyn Dodgers (now based in L.A.), and the Montreal Royals went into the history books. (Incidentally, Chuck Conners, The Rifleman, played first base and hit a home run.)

I've encountered blacks many times since—my thesis advisor, for example, is both black and a member of the National Academy of Science—but never in large numbers. Put me in a crowded alleyway in Lagos or Harlem or South Central L.A. and I'm sure the same thing would happen as happened that afternoon in Fort Lee.

I panicked.

Without penetrating farther into the town, I turned the car about and headed back the way I'd come, toward the Interstate and a geography and ethnicity I understood. I changed the Stones tape for the Doors. My Nissan passed beneath I-95 and immediately I was in familiar territory: tract homes, a K-mart, a Home Depot; power lawn mowers and trash compactors. The people who lived here might be Klansman, Jew haters and white supremacists, they might not have my politics, or my culture, but they were white and I would be safe among them.

Truthfully, the town, Pineville, also was a place President Benjamin of Benjamin College had recommended. "You may find Pineville a bit more like the towns you're used to up North. The electronic plant on the outskirts has attracted a lot of people like yourself."

"We should get jobs for our students there," I suggested.

"We should," President Benjamin agreed with a chuckle, "and maybe you're the man to make the connection. Yes, I believe you are. So check out the Pineville area. You can live in Fort Lee adjacent to the campus as many of our faculty do, but I think you may just find Pineville the town of your choice."

My choice was Pineville: Small enough I would meet people quickly. Big enough no one would pay any special attention to me. Restaurants that served something besides fried chicken; chain stores that competed on price and selection. If Pineville, like Fort Lee, held no concert halls, theaters or museums, Atlanta was only an hour and a half away.

Waking late in my motel room the next morning, I was confronted by the same seven tasks that face all of us when we move to a new area: Find an apartment and a way to be reached by telephone; get the gas and lights turned on; locate a well-stocked, inexpensive grocery store, a cleaners that can be trusted, a shoemaker, too, and a new friend of the sex of our choice.

I was able to take care of three of my concerns—a room, an answering service, and a girl friend—with a single stop.

An answering service was essential if I was to keep on with my job search. Propping myself up next to the restrooms in the coffee shop with a ballpoint, a stack of dimes and the yellow pages turned to "Ambulance—Answering," I began a series of calls. Two stacks of dimes later, the margins were covered with prices. Each service had its own method of billing, its own complicated set of options. I could have flipped a coin. Instead, I did what I always do in these situations and opted for the service with the friendliest receptionist.

The short blond woman who welcomed me to Ansa-Pine, seemed somewhat vague about the details I needed. "You'll have to ask Joann," she kept repeating in slow, almost dull-witted fashion.

"And what's your name?" I asked, hoping this might put her at her ease.

"Peri." Her strong rural accent induced a strange set of conflicting emotions. Her face was so right for me, her accent and her mannerisms were so wrong.

"My name is Peter."

"You're not from around here."

"I just got to town."

She gazed at me intently as if searching for the content of my character. I gazed back. Undeniably attractive, though a far cry from any women I'd dated. Small firm breasts, held proudly almost arrogantly, and a narrow waist that flared out at the hips; short, tiny-boned, almost frail, with a way of cocking her head on one side like a bird as she talked. She didn't appear to be wearing any makeup, and didn't need it, I thought. Her eyes were a lively blue, somewhat careworn. Her hair was a sort of dishwater blond with a perm that hadn't quite taken; stray locks would uncurl suddenly and fall forward across her face; she pushed them back with her tiny fingers, but they always fell forward again.

To get a date with a girl, you first have to ask her. "You are very beautiful," I said to Peri.

"Are you a doctor?" she asked ignoring my words. All right, so what I'd said sounded like and was a line. But how else could I force a beginning?

"A doctor? Why do you think that?"

"The way you talk."

Her last word, "talk," was drawled, impossibly long. For an instant, I thought she might be making fun of me. Weren't we city slickers always fair game? "Not exactly a doctor," I replied, "I mean I have a Ph.D. But I'm a professor and an administrator."

"That's nice," she said, a woefully inadequate reply, almost a put down, yet when Joann returned, "He's a professor," were the first words out of Peri's lips.

Joann was all business. "Have you been waiting long?"

Wanting to protect Peri, I said no, I'd just got there. Peri, in her turn, said I'd been waiting for at least fifteen minutes. Amused by the inconsistency, Joann's full red lips curled in a smile; she asked if there were any questions she might answer. But I'd already made my decision. "I'll buy the service," I said, "And is it all right if I take your secretary to lunch?"

Peri gave me a strange look. "You haven't asked me yet."

I smiled at her. "Will you go to lunch with me?" And so began my relationship with the second most important person in my life.

At lunch with Peri—Joann had taken only a few minutes to get the details of billing and payment arranged—I repeated that I'd just arrived in town, taught at Benjamin College, and was looking for a place to live. "You could live with me," Peri said, "Can you pay your share of the rent?"

I said I could pay both our shares.

She gave me another of those penetrating stares. "You're pretty forward."

"You're pretty attractive," I replied.

She snorted, not exactly overawed. "Well, I've two bedrooms. My girlfriend just moved out. Maybe for now, you could sleep in one of the bedrooms and I could sleep in the other."

I didn't say any of a half dozen clever and not-so-clever things, but let it alone, satisfied I would be near this attractive engaging woman, whatever living relationship we came up with.

Peri seemed quite casual about giving her house key to an almost total stranger. I telephoned her anyway as soon as I unloaded my car, both to reassure her I was going ahead with the plan and to ask for her suggestions for a dry cleaner and a shoemaker.

Directions in hand, I headed out almost immediately from the small two-bedroom cottage in which she lived, first to the grocery store—I would try to buy my own stuff and not impose—and then to drop my suits and dress pants off at the cleaners. My suits had not done well in my automobile trunk; they'd started out on top, but had gradually worked their way toward the bottom as a result of a series of after-dark retrievals.

The supermarket was fascinating, new smells, new products. I have a tendency inherited from my mother to linger in grocery stores, to look at each of the fruits and vegetables as if seeing them for the first time. I bought beets, lettuce, parsnips, and green peppers. And a bag of squishy boiled peanuts, from a vendor on the sidewalk outside the store. I'd never eaten boiled peanuts before (and may not again; they are an acquired taste), but they smelled wonderful. I also bought strawberries and a fresh pineapple from which the outer husk had been removed. Moving-in gifts for Peri.

When I emerged from the supermarket, raindrops spattered from the pavement and awnings. Not a cool rain, which would have been delightful given the hot sultry afternoon, but a warm rain that only made me feel hotter and stickier.

Suddenly, I realized I was afraid to go back to Peri's cottage, scared that barriers would suddenly appear, my key would not fit, the girlfriend who had moved out would return to displace me, or Peri herself would reappear and say, "I'm sorry but I've changed my mind."

I pushed through the rain and fear, and then, miracle of miracles, the door opened to my key, no message of dismissal awaited me within, and the sky cleared long enough for me to move the groceries and the last few remaining items from my car.

I had offered and, in fact, was looking forward to taking Peri out to dinner, but she surprised and pleased me by offering to cook for us both. "I don't cook often," she said, "living alone and all. That's why I'm just skin and bone. I'd like to cook for you, for the two of us."

"Thank you."

"How's the room?" she asked changing the subject, abruptly. I hoped I would soon adapt to the way her mind leaped from topic to topic.

"Quite large," I said, "I'm going to go looking for a bed tomorrow. Oh, and do you have an extra book shelf?"

"There's no bed?" she repeated, fixing on the first thing I had told her. She sounded surprised.

"No. The room's pretty bare; maybe that's why it looks so large." I laughed nervously.

"She was supposed to leave the bed. My girlfriend," she continued, when I looked puzzled.

"No. No bed. I can sleep on the couch." I pointed to the piece of furniture in question, though I was actually planning to sleep on the floor for the sake of my back and improvise a mattress from the couch cushions.

"Best eat." she said tersely, putting the problem aside. Dinner was ready. Peri had used the vegetables I bought that afternoon, though she surprised me by keeping the greens I would have discarded and cooking and serving these separately. They tasted as delicious as the beets and parsnips themselves, and with the addition of some ham, which she took from her side of the refrigerator, we had a perfectly wonderful meal. Oh, and we had biscuits, homemade ones, not the heat-and-serve-in-a-tin kind that I buy. "I really like strawberries," she said, and she whipped up some cream she found in the back of the refrigerator—"my girlfriend's"—to put on top.

Bedtime was awkward. At the last moment, Peri suggested I sleep in her bedroom, each of us on our own side of the bed. "Can you be trusted?" she asked.

"What do you mean?" I replied.

"If I let you sleep next to me, will you stay on your side of the bed?"

"Yes, I suppose. Yes, of course."

I didn't volunteer a second time to sleep out in the living room. I wanted to be next to her. And if I'd never before spent the night in a bed next to a beautiful woman without touching her, well, not since I was seventeen, it would still be fun even if I lie awake all night.

I slept though, immediately and deeply. Who wouldn't after waking up at six a.m. for a final cross-country dash, driving in the rain, along a backcountry road through south-central Georgia and West Africa, finding a cottage, unpacking the car. . . .

In the middle of the night, it began to rain again. I woke, went to the toilet to urinate, then carefully slipped back in bed beside Peri. What would happen, I wondered, if I were to try to make love to her? Her back was to me, my nose buried in her hair, and I slipped my arms around her, my hands on her breasts, cuddling her rump with my loins, two spoons in a drawer. Her hair smelled of seaweed, the smell of the sea. I heard the rain falling; I felt tremendously grateful she had not moved when I placed my arms around her, but had left her small firm breasts in my hands, her nipples pressing out against my fingers.

When I woke again, it had stopped raining. The air in the room was unexpectedly cool. I shivered, reached for my shirt and put it on over my shoulders, leaving it unbuttoned.

Peri was turned toward me, her face as calm and peaceful as the face of a sleeping child; a slight hint of moisture gave her cheeks a sheen that glowed in the pre-dawn light. Without thinking, I reached out and clasped her to me in a thoroughly fatherly hug. And then—no denying the movement, though, unexpected, it took me completely by surprise, her loins began to grind against mine. "Peri?" I whispered softly; I heard no reply; she might still be asleep.

Asleep or awake, the movements of her hips continued, until my own rising excitement could no longer be concealed. I felt her moist softness against the tip of my penis. When had she taken off her panties? Hadn't she had them on when we first slipped in bed together? "Peri?" She sighed, reached up and kissed me lightly on the lips. I kissed her back and then, as easily if we had been making love all of our lives, I slipped inside her.

Chapter 5.

I reached the Benjamin campus that morning, my reluctance and all the false turns I made not withstanding. I did my best to procrastinate, deliberately refusing to use the map, relying on nonexistent and faded and fallen guideposts. The road cooperated—flagmen pointed me on unfamiliar detours, long trains took their tea breaks on the tracks before me—but my watch would not go along with the delays. Well before nine a.m., my Nissan slipped into a parking spot adjacent to the campus and a short walk guaranteed to bring me to my new office.

Little did I realize it would be weeks before my office was actually assigned and I had many, many stations to visit that day before, weary, I could finally put my feet up on a borrowed desk.

My guide for the first part of my journey was a fellow Berkeleyite, Associate Dean Merrill Jefferson. Like me, a department head, and like me, not a particularly outstanding Cal alumnus, which explained our common presence, here and now, at Benjamin University.

Despite the heat, already rising in great waves from the pavement, Merrill wore a three-piece suit of some wool-rayon mixture. French cuffs displayed studs of the familiar Berkeley blue and gold and his tie had been carefully knotted as if he had no intention of removing it at the first reasonable opportunity. "I'm glad you accepted our offer," he said by way of greeting, first a wave from across the parking lot, then a clap on my shoulder and a pumping hand, "We need more scholars."

Merrill had adopted me at the initial interview, carrying on as if he had invited me to the campus in the first place, (as indeed he had, I found out later), remarking over and over about our years together at Berkeley, though we'd overlapped for only one of them, his first and my last in graduate school. We'd once spent 24 hours together, he said, part of a hodgepodge of students barricaded on the second floor of the Berkeley Administration Building. I don't remember him—though I do remember the long sleepless night and the endless hours spent in court, later—but he insists he remembers me.

Classes were not scheduled to start until the following day, yet parking lots were filled and sidewalks overflowed with chattering students—all black—standing in noisy expectant groups wherever shade was available.

The hairs on the back of my neck rose automatically; too many blacks, too close. Fortunately, Merrill was on hand to guide me through and passed them to the first meeting of the day, the Welcome Ceremony.

I sat uncomfortably in the center of the third row—Merrill's choice. Around us, the crowd—aging faculty to the front, freshmen and sophomore-transfer students to the rear—exchanged shouted greetings and walked up and down the aisles. While I hunched in my chair, Merrill remained on his feet for twenty minutes or so, pumping hands, until the stage began to fill with personage after personage and the last black head ceased to twist about in conversation with its neighbor and focus on the platform.

First of the speakers to rise from his chair next to the dais was Bobbi Walsh, head of the Alumni Association. With his checkered vest and fluttery mannerisms, Walsh looked more like my conception of Sporting Life than the CEO of a large cosmetics firm. After some fifteen minutes of platitudes, he introduced A.O. Benjamin, the president of Benjamin College. The audience, which had chattered all through Walsh's speech, grew silent.

President Benjamin introduced new members of the faculty and I got to stand for all of ten seconds while applause went on around me. Next to speak—at times it seemed the dais was as filled with people as the auditorium itself—was Martin King, the unctuous and somewhat disoriented president of the student body, followed by Royce Parker and Kitisha Thomas, student heads, male and female, respectively, of the PanHellenic Societies, and, last, Beau-Beau Lee, the Vice-President of Academic Affairs.

The President spoke briefly and effectively—I had been impressed with him from our very first meeting—college was good; college was a challenge the students must rise to meet; they would be the better for the hurdles. Bobbi Walsh and Martin King sounded the same welcoming note, Royce and Kitisha preened, Beau-Beau Lee spoke on and on.

Beau-Beau, in fact, went a bridge too far. Discussing at length an unspecified situation that had occurred the previous year, he said to the students, "I may be an administrator but I'm your friend, too. If you have problems with your professors, come see me."

The students burst into wild applause; the faculty sat in stunned silence. We knew that problems with professors meant only one thing: grades. Was Beau-Beau planning to dumb-down our grade sheets, alter them behind our backs, or, worse, have us acquiesce to administration-imposed grade changes? President Benjamin had asked the students to rise to the challenge; Beau-Beau was telling them he'd lower the hurdles. Not for the last time, I was to wonder who really was in charge at Benjamin College.

After the meeting, Merrill introduced me to a half dozen of my new colleagues, all male and, like Merrill, all black. They said they were pleased to see me, but after a cursory glance at my clothing, they began talking among themselves. The conversation focused on the innocuous: how I spent my summer vacation, who had come back, who was teaching elsewhere, and featured a host of names of people and places with which I was not familiar. Nothing about Beau-Beau Lee and his rash promises. Nothing about a newcomer from California who could have used five minutes or so of individual attention. I walked away neglected, though I was one of the few, the very few white faces in the auditorium.

At my departmental office, an indifferent secretary barely glanced up at me. Returning to her paperback, Mz. Washington (according to the half-concealed name plate) informed me the former chairperson had not yet vacated "her," soon-to-be "my" office, the Dean (not yet in) might know where my temporary office was located, and I had better get a parking sticker before I did anything else.

I was dispatched to security (for my parking sticker) and, on my own, peeked in at the library and the gym. Each stop required I meet new people, and be the subject of an embarrassing and detailed inspection. If more than one person were behind the counter, they would often take to discussing me as if I weren't in the room. "He walk funny," was an oft-repeated comment.

Stubby maples, magnolias, ornamental peaches, and a few tall pecans dotted the campus, but all paths seemed to lie in bright intense sunlight, so that I was soon sweating and uncomfortable. Again, I wondered why everyone around me was so overdressed. In Pineville, short sleeves and causal pants were the dress of the day;

at Benjamin College, only a few miles and a civilization away, the men wore three-piece suits—Merrill was the rule not the exception—and the women, long dresses like characters in a turn-of-the-century play.

If I'd found my first glimpse of the greater University community depressing and unnerving, my initial meeting with my own department later that morning made me want to cut and run.

First to introduce himself was Mr. Singh, two of them I think, equally gracious, equally blank-faced, equally incomprehensible; then came the bespectacled Mr. Sun, quite bright possibly, had his limited knowledge of English been up to communicating his brightness; Oxford-educated Professor Boourassa, our senior chemistry lecturer, admitted he might well be out of touch with more modern laboratory methods; wispy Mr. Fraser's slight frame was lost in a brown cashmere sweater which would have looked better on the slender young woman which I'm sure he longed to be; and, last to be recognized, Ms. Samanahapathabana, a pretty, extremely shy girl from Thailand, blushed and sat down after only a few inaudible words.

An elegantly attired 30ish black man slipped into a chair at the back of the room. Raymond White, I guessed, glancing down at the slip in my hand. White might well have stepped from the pages of Gentleman's Quarterly with his stylish suit, vest and hand-painted tie. How he withstood the heat was a mystery. Though I'd not done much more than carry my suit jacket about, I was perspiring heavily and longed for the opportunity to slip into my own air-conditioned office and loosen my tie. But White was to look as immaculate at the end of the meeting as he had at the start. He declined my proffered hand and, while other members of the faculty struggled to ingratiate themselves, stared straight ahead, indifferent and impervious.

"You don't have to keep any of them on if you don't want to," my Dean told me, when I remarked on this odd collection to him later that day, "except Mrs. Black, of course. None of them have contracts."

I grunted my surprise. Most universities would have issued contracts five or six months before the new term started.

"We told them we'd let the new man make the assignments." The Dean's tone implied Benjamin faculty seldom got the opportunity to bargain.

"So, I can get rid of all of them?" I repeated, begging for confirmation. I could not believe my good fortune.

"Just make sure you have their replacements. Oh, and I should tell you if I haven't already, both Mr. White, he used to be Dr. White, and Mrs. Black will have to be retained." I couldn't see the Dean's face when he said this—our entire conversation took place over the telephone—but I imagine his smile may have shown a great many teeth.

"Mrs. Black?" I questioned; no such person had appeared at that morning's meeting.

"She used to be the chairperson; she'll only be teaching part time from now on, so she really won't get in your way."

"Is she the one in my office?" I inquired calmly.

The Dean fairly gushed his apologies, "I thought she'd already left. I am sorry about that. We'll find something for you."

I didn't believe him. I know Deans didn't like subordinates who contradict them, but I had to say something. "Soon," I ventured.

"Soon."

"And Mr., uh Dr. White?" I persisted, remembering those hate stares vividly.

"Yes, he used to be chairperson, also, until we found out he really didn't have a doctorate. Your own papers are in order, of course?" Was the Dean still smiling as he said this?

"Of course," I replied.

The lady in personnel, a buxom, rather attractive white woman named Mrs. Veronica Angel looked at me with sad, soulful eyes and verified everything the Dean had told me. "Oh yes. It's completely up to you which faculty you retain. Would be a pity about Mr. Sun, though."

"Yes?" I said, my deep for-women-only voice filled with feigned concern. My interest was limited to Mrs. Angel herself; her full rich mouth seemed designed for long kisses.

"Immigration may send him back to China."

I promised Mrs. Angel I would "see," a meaningless bureaucratic phrase that seemed to comfort her. To me, the key issue was not what became of those I let go, but whether I could get replacements for them on such short notice. "Do we have applications for these jobs?" I asked.

"Hundreds. I'm sort of grateful I can turn these files over to you. Mr. White..." her voice dropped before she continued, "wasn't too organized."

"He wasn't a doctor either, I gather."

She shook her head. "By the way, do you have your, uh, official transcripts?"

An awkward moment for both of us. I didn't have my transcripts with me, of course—"I didn't know I was supposed to bring them"—but I could understand why she would need to see them; they would provide proof of my doctorate, as would the framed copy of my doctoral diploma, still at the bottom of my suitcase. "I'll bring them tomorrow." I added.

"That would be fine," she said, sounding relieved.

We looked at each other for a moment, two white faces in a sea of black, trying to see through and below the surface. I returned to reality first, "Is there an office with a phone I could use?" Mrs. Angel looked doubtful, no less so after I had explained about the Dean and Mrs. Black and my own missing office, but pointed me toward a desk in the middle of the room.

Half a dozen black women including several student workers looked on and listened as I made my calls. With so many listening, my faculty was sure to be aware by the end of the day of my plans for replacing them.

It didn't take that long. The Singhs and Mr. Sun took me to lunch where each stammered an oath of loyalty, need, and desperation. Ms. Samanahapathabana drew me into her office and burst into tears without producing a single meaningful utterance.

My phone calls continued after lunch and by three Eastern time, I had a new faculty: A UCLA physics Ph.D. was rescued by my job offer from two years on his girlfriend's living-room couch. ("I'm not his girlfriend," she insisted later when we met.) A distinguished chemist of Persian descent had spent a year in Tehran but "couldn't stand the government listening in on every part of my life." He'd returned to the USA, jobless, and I snapped him up for a third of his former salary.

Junk bond salesmen make millions, and high-energy physicists sleep on their girlfriend's couches. I'm sure some kind of moral can be elicited by the more discerning. My successful oldest daughter, the Ayn Rand disciple, would say, without a hint of compassion, that such displacement is the inevitable result of market forces. My friend Ed, also a UCLA Ph.D., switched from physics to real estate ten years ago and made a fortune. He still writes equations on the back of cocktail napkins and between deals has been known to publish articles in theoretical physics. I prefer to teach myself, remain on the edge of poverty (or will as long as I have three daughters in college), and am a sad and angry man.

But the day was not over. Still without a place to put my belongings, I heard my name called as I walked by the department office. The departmental secretary, Mz. Washington, emerged, moving slowly and painfully, dragging one leg after her as if it were crippled and deformed. (Later, I learned this manner of slow walking was an idiosyncrasy that vanished each day just before quitting time.) "I's got stuff for you to sign." (Her slow, southern manner of speaking was also a mannerism, for she had started her life in Chicago, had a degree as a speech therapist, and somehow, through incredible miscalculation had ended up working for minuscule pay on our backwoods campus. Or maybe it wasn't a miscalculation, but the certain knowledge she would need only provide a half-day's work here for the half-day's pay.)

Mz. W had a pile of stuff, indeed, mainly student petitions, for me to sign. "But these are for the Dean," I protested, referring to that absent personage, Dean Holley, my boss, whom I'd met only by telephone.

"He say they fo' you from now on. You in charg'."

"Then oughtn't I to have an office?" But my sarcasm was lost on her; too near quitting time, I suppose.

I started to leaf through the buff-colored forms, each bearing the plaintive tale of some student who believed that he or she had been dreadfully wronged. "I'm not sure I know how to be in charge," I confided.

"Best you see Miss Feret."

I gave her a questioning look.

"She the Dean." No further information forthcoming, I went in search of Ms. Feret; what else could I do, prop my feet up on a borrowed desk?

Another person, another building. Miss Feret was young, for a Dean of Students, with an eye-riveting bosom and a loose, yet somehow form-fitting blouse. Thick bottle-cap lenses marred what would otherwise have been a perfect face. She was black, of course, but on the cafe au lait side; as I glanced at her, I knew I was more than willing to abandon all prejudice.

(And what about Peri, I hear my female readers complain, angered by my roving eye. Give me a break, will you; as far as this book goes, Peri and I just met. We may have slept together, but it's not as if we had the eighteen years and three children I had with my ex.)

"I'm not sure, I understand these forms," I said.

"Let me see if I can help you." Dean Feret's voice was cheery, bright, and she sounded as if she meant the offer. She didn't trouble to ask who I was, probably because I was one of the few white people on campus. Then, too, I'd been asked to stand up, albeit briefly, at the President's welcome meeting that morning. She'd noted my presence; I took this as a promising sign.

"Well, if I were you..." she began.

"Please," I interjected, "Be me for awhile, at least until I get on my feet."

"Ohh. Kay." she said, beginning to leaf through the petitions, "This one, I'd probably say 'yes;' Kisha really did have a death in the family and all she wants to do is repeat the course. If you like, I'll even make a notation that she doesn't have to pay a second time."

I nodded my happiness.

"This one, I'd probably say 'no.' Larrine's got a habit of sitting in on courses without paying and then enrolling at the last minute only if she is sure of passing. This time she wants to register for a course she took last spring. Pretty strange."

"I'll just put 'no'." I suggested.

Ms. Ferret leaned her bosom over the paper in front of me, shedding perfume and her own natural aroma as she did so, and pointed to the box I needed to check. "'Denied' is the official term we use here. Oh, and write a reason too in this space, something like, eh, 'too late to enroll.'"

I did as she instructed on each of the petitions and in the end was left with only three of the buff-colored forms. "Why don't I put them aside for another day?" I said and ventured, "It will give us time to go out for a coffee break."

"No thank you," she replied crisply; our business, regretfully, was at an end; "I've got a whole stack of petitions of my own to attend to and, unlike you, I don't have a secretary."

Later, much later, I realized this last remark might be construed as having fun at my expense. Mz. Washington, my department secretary, was both a notorious non-worker and a close friend of the enchanting Miss Ferret. Mz. W's chief value, the one that secured her position, was not to me but to others; in later weeks, she could be counted on to find me with bad news wherever I hid.

But this discovery lies in the future. That afternoon, I made my way to the parking lot, waved to a departing Mrs. Angel—what a heavenly bosom—and to two total strangers who waved to me, and bugged out. My first, utterly exhausting day on campus was over.

Chapter 6.

I received a welcome phone call from my oldest daughter today. Peri brought a stack of messages home with her. One was from my mother, who merely needed to be reassured I was alive and well and prospering and would call her soon. Peri said, almost her first words when I walked through the cottage door, "I talked to your mother this morning; she sounded like a nice lady."

"Did you tell her we were living together?" I asked, facetiously.

Peri wrinkled her nose, "No, of course not."

The other calls were from my daughter and from a former and perhaps prospective client. I thanked Peri for bringing me the messages. "A special service," she said reaching up to me on tiptoe to be kissed, "along with preparing you a special meal to celebrate your first day on your new job."

My face revealed my pleasure. Her gift was as welcome and as unexpected as our lovemaking the night before. I'd thought about dinner or, rather, my stomach had, for the past hour or so, but I'd still been thinking in terms of truck stops and coffee shops. Nothing could be more satisfying than to find a fragrant home-cooked meal on my own table.

"I cooked up the vegetables you brought home, and I fixed us some fish and some okra too." Again I felt, however often I said thank-you to Peri, my thanks would be inadequate to express my gratitude. (I cleared the table after dinner, washed the dishes, and swept the kitchen floor. I'd learned something from the wreckage of my first marriage.)

Samantha, my oldest daughter and the one of my three with whom I am on most intimate terms, was at home when I returned her call. We exchanged pleasantries: she was doing well, loved her room in the senior dorm—I'd talked her out of moving into an apartment for her final year—and wanted to know how her dad was getting on.

I shared with her not only the events of the day but some of my feelings, the most prominent of which was the knowledge the hairs on the back of my neck stood up each time I found myself surrounded by a group of black students.

"Does that happen often?"

"Constantly. It's an all-black campus. I hope I'll get used to it."

She made a clicking sound with her tongue in imitation of her mother. "You're not used to blacks, Dad."

"No, I'm not. I'm going to have to get used to them or take cortisone or something to cut down the stress. I'm not the only white on the faculty though. I've heard a couple of married ladies are on the staff, one married to a black, the other to a professor at the white university."

"What's the white university?" The puzzlement in my daughter's voice echoed my own curiosity earlier that day.

"Another branch of the State University is in Murphesborough about forty-five minutes from here. Both campuses are integrated, in theory, but the fact is the blacks go here and the whites go there, even if both groups have to get on the highway for a couple of hours each day."

"Cool."

"Perhaps."

"Who answered the phone today, Dad?" Samantha does seem to zoom in quickly on the sensitive areas. I could hear Peri moving about in the kitchen—was she redoing the dishes I'd washed so carefully?

"Answering service." I replied deflecting the question.

"Good idea. Got any clients yet?"

"Couple of nibbles. I'll be able to cover your second-semester tuition."

"Don't sweat it; the school is giving me another scholarship."

God, I was proud.

"I'm the Libertarian merit scholar."

I shook my head in mock laughter. Her politics and mine are far apart, but, hey, if they won her a scholarship.

"I could use seventy-five dollars for brake pads, though."

A job for super-Dad, a chance to be a hero to my daughter once more, "Check is in the mail. The life of a Libertarian scholar is cheap at half the price."

"Thanks, Dad."

When I hung up and saw Peri standing in the shadows at the far end of the hallway, I thought of what I hadn't said to my daughter: A new person has entered my life. She was meant to be just someone I dated and slept with. Now, it seems she might be turning into something more.

I wanted to tell Peri all about Samantha, and Marilyn and Diana my other daughters. About Samantha's successes and Diana's problems. But Peri didn't ask and I was reluctant to ramble on about my children, not knowing if Peri had children of her own, not really knowing much about the person I lived with.

I will tell her about my other daughters later, I thought, and if I am still living with her two or three months from now, then I will tell my daughters about her, too.

Phone call completed, I had the rest of the evening to get through. Never an easy thing for me unless I've got something to do. I'm a Type A person, more or less, and have yet to learn to deal with or justify rest and relaxation. (Dr. Berman again: We are doing regression therapy and I am inside my mother's womb.

"Can you hear your mother?"

"Yes." My voice, calm and detached, comes from outside of me.

"What is she saying?"

"She is thinking her mother will be so proud of her now that she has this child.")

I'd done the dishes—and did them again, Peri had fixed us a quick dessert—vanilla pudding—while I was on the telephone. Now, I helped to make the bed, realizing with a pang as I tucked in the sheets, smelling slightly of the potpourri Peri stored with them, that this was something I should have done by myself before I left for work that morning.

We kissed when we met tucking in a corner. Could we make love now? How much, if anything, could I take for granted?

"We just made the bed," she said. "But I will if you want to." I pulled her down to sit beside me on the half-made bed. We kissed a second time, a long moist revealing kiss. I pulled her blouse loose from her skirt and reached up to unhook her bra. "Turn off the light," she said.

7:38 p.m. read the bedside clock. What now, I thought, looking up at the ceiling. My work at school hadn't really begun; regular classes wouldn't start until Monday. No lectures to prepare for or papers to correct. "Movie? T.V.?" I called out to Peri, who I could hear moving about in the next room.

"Whatever you want to do," came the reply. We took the briefest of walks around the neighborhood—a park only a block and a half from her cottage offered swings and a small group of trees where lovers could get lost among the paths—and then went to bed and made love a second time.

Friday, the second and last day of orientation, was as exhausting as Thursday had been, with perhaps, Peri excepted, less to look forward to. Again, the after-supper love making, though this time she let me study and caress her breasts at length before she turned out the light. Rising from bed, strangely exhilarated, we again strolled along the maze of streets that led from our small enclave of cottages to the park.

"Stars," she said, looking up into the night sky, "Do you know about stars?"

Some, I thought, as trivial bits of information about stellar evolution, white dwarfs and black holes came back to me.

"What's that star called?"

Bright, unwinking, a planet not a star. Too late in the evening to be Venus. "Jupiter." I replied, "A planet not a star."

"Our star," she said.

The next morning, Saturday, I suggested she might want to go with me that afternoon to the football game, the first of the season for Benjamin.

"No," was all she said. And though the game was only a short distance away—Benjamin was using Pineville High's stadium, for some inexplicable reason—I spent Saturday afternoon and evening alone, for she was "out" when I returned.

Sunday was another day of uncertainty.

We'd made love that morning, twice, shortly after midnight, when, waking, I discovered her cuddled at my side, and again an hour or two after the sun rose, after I'd closed the blind and windows and turned on the air-conditioning. So that part of my life was still certain, steady. But what about the other part, where Peri and I did things together as persons, as friends? What did one do in Pineville on Sunday, anyway?

One went to church. If one was Peri, one didn't force church on the other person—though her conduct in this respect was very much the exception in both Pineville and Fort Valley.

"I might have wanted to go with you," I said to Peri. She'd slipped off while I was sleeping, and I'd woken to an empty cottage. "I made lunch," I added.

"I'll join you," she said, "though I already had something to eat at Church afterwards."

"What kind of church is it?" I asked her later, foreseeing that sooner or later we would go there together.

"Baptist."

I'd been to church before, in another time and another place. Working one summer in Houston, it seemed the only dates I could get were to escort a young lady to services. The Baptists favored simple hymns and long-winded sermons, heavy on heaven and hell, light on practical guidance to the Peaceable Kingdom of day-to-day living. A pamphlet in one congregation's lobby read, "Many Jews do not realize the Southern Baptist loves them. Many Southern Baptists do not realize this either."

Each service ended with an impassioned plea to come forward and surrender to the Lord. The organ would play, the choir sing lustily, and then one, two, even three bewildered souls would come forward to meet their creator and a welcoming committee from the Baptist Fellowship. Invariably, the poor man (or woman) would prove to be the victim of demon rum—this was in the years before crack cocaine—and in return for his or her confession would receive meal tickets and the price of a flop. On occasion, I was in a position to reveal that a recent candidate for redemption had attained enlightenment the previous week at a different bastion of the Christian faith, but to do so would have led to intricate not-to-be-ventured explanations as to how and with whom I had come to be at that other church in the first place.

Having experienced my own epiphany some years before, and joined the Religious Society of Friends, the risk I foresaw in going again to a Baptist church with Peri was that I might try to recruit parishioners to my own faith. I warned Peri of this possibility, but she only said, "Don't be silly," and I saw that our joint appearance at her church was inevitable.

(And why not, I can hear my female readers asking. She's your woman isn't she? Yes, and I her man.)

Sunday afternoon, we lie about the house, the Atlanta Constitution forming a patchwork about my feet, while Peri remained content with a paperback she'd brought home from work. We made love of course, and walked again to the nearby park once the long shadows of the afternoon had contained the sun. But we did not discuss what we believed and why or where our dreams were carrying us.

Chapter 7.

My subsequent days were busy ones.

"You'll find plenty of challenges," President Benjamin had told me at my initial interview, and he was right.

Some of these challenges were external: Benjamin College had a reputation for turning out less-than-qualified students and I had to change that image if our graduates were to find jobs. But the vast majority of our problems were internal and well under our control, that is, if someone in power had cared to make the commitment.

The students were ill prepared, a result of our open-admissions policy. So, too, were many of the faculty. I would endure the first—I had no choice, and I had begun to correct the second. The Singhs were gone and Mr. Sun was in Atlanta arguing with the Immigration Service.

Our distinctly second-rate administrators, failed offspring of the system they'd pledged to rebuild, were reluctant to make changes. They'd succeeded, hadn't they? (And just maybe they heard footsteps, feared a better-educated generation would displace them.)

Beau-Beau Lee, our Academic Vice President, was a prime example of this internal contradiction: At the inaugural meeting of the Faculty Senate—compulsory for all faculty—Beau-Beau launched into an hour-long harangue, reminiscent of Nixon at his worst, with little room offered for conflicting opinions or common sense.

We were encouraged as a group to seek outside monies for the school, while being admonished for overburdening secretaries and Xerox machines. Even someone like myself, a new boy on the block who hadn't had time to be guilty of anything, came in for criticism. "I'll be talking to you about broken glassware," Beau Beau warned, as if, somehow, student breakage in the laboratories had become my personal responsibility.

Surprisingly, a tall bespectacled gray-haired Negro spoke out on my behalf, using more or less the same arguments to defend me that I would have used myself. "Who's he?" I asked Merrill Jefferson as he slid into the seat next to me.

As always, Merrill's clothing was immaculate even at the end of the day, while my own beige short-sleeved shirt dripped with perspiration. "That's your boss, Dean Holley," Merrill replied with some astonishment. "You haven't met him?"

And of course, I hadn't, though I'd heard from him on several occasions via Mz. W and had spoken to him twice on the telephone.

After the meeting, I rushed over to talk with the Dean, but was too late, he was already deep in conversation with Beau Beau and other senior administrators. He gave me a friendly nod, but did not interrupt his conversation to greet me. I stood to for a while, then drifted among a number of small groups of which I was not really a part. On my return circuit of the room, he'd disappeared.

Perhaps, I wasn't as important as I thought I was. Though, on the day of my job interview, President Benjamin left me with the impression I was his personal choice, "The man who could help turn things around at Benjamin." He never actually followed up on our discussion, but I always thought he might, someday when he had the time.

Seemingly our President was everywhere, chairing this and that committee, addressing a series of student and parent gatherings, from a special "Freshman Welcoming," in which I had a brief and inexplicable part—"Hello. I'm the new chair of Health Sciences, a program offering innumerable opportunities for tomorrow's graduates," to Alpha Chi Alpha's welcome mixer which the President attended both as head of the University and as an alum.

President Benjamin, if I may digress for a moment, tended to bring a fixed set of views to our committee meetings. While he always thanked everyone for their contributions, the real decisions seemed to be being made behind closed doors. At best our shared gatherings were an occasion for posturing on the part of the higher ups. Like gorillas in some legendary planet of the ages, Beau-Beau Lee, the Registrar, and the Vice-President for Long Range Planning, would take turns pounding their chests and extolling the simple virtues.

Occasionally the meeting would be interrupted as someone from accounting or the comptroller's office entered the room. The President would halt in mid peroration to sign a paper or examine some note that seemed to require his immediate attention. Afterward, the direction of the meeting would change abruptly. A plan on the verge of adoption would be set aside, an item that had been the source of contentious debate would be forgotten, replaced by a brand new topic.

My Dean spoke seldom, and usually only to echo the opinion of Beau-Beau Lee, the Vice President to whom he reported.

My Dean could and should have spoken out. Almost retired—witness our many and varied telephone conversations that originated from his home—he had virtually nothing to lose by a display of initiative.

We needed initiative. We were a no-pride, no-name, no-money institution with, I guessed (correctly), a whole series of skeletons just waiting to be unearthed.

But my Dean had not reached his middling academic rank—two steps above my own—by rash action. The habits of a lifetime were not easily broken, except by the occasional wry smile, a wink, or even an under-the-breath comment for only us loyal subordinates—Merrill and myself—to hear.

I wanted to break the silence, to speak out and be recognized—because the system needed changing, because, insecure, I needed to be at the center of things.

As a reward for my own attendance, I was allowed, even expected as the token white (or token scientist), to provide one comment per meeting. This proved to be an advantage when the problem was a pressing one like our aging and unsafe physics and chemistry laboratories. But too many things were wrong in my department, too many changes had to be effected.

The conditions I'd inherited were shocking. They included ill-equipped, unsafe laboratories, few visual aids, and course syllabuses and catalog descriptions that seldom reflected actual content. Though my new faculty had gone to work with a zeal that astonished even a born-again Type A like me, it would take us some time to regroup and reorganize. Meanwhile, I had to come up with a plan that would make the best of what we did have.

My solution was to try to rebuild the program a year at a time, and I said as much to my faculty, those who bothered to attend my meetings, "Four years from now our department will be a center of excellence." But it was the faculty members who didn't attend or contribute, the faculty members I wasn't allowed to replace, Mrs. Black and Mr. White, who stood in the way of my plans.

Mrs. Black taught whatever she wanted, to whomever she wanted, regardless of course descriptions and, sometimes, of enrollment. She was rumored to have great powers as a fixer, and her students actually believed that taking her course, Botany 200, would give them credit for mine, Anatomy 206. (Not so naively, I found out that year at commencement; several seniors somehow satisfied departmental requirements by repeating Botany 200 three times!)

As I was not allowed to replace her, the only solution seemed to be to try to match what she taught with her course assignments, rather than the more traditional course-assignment-first, lecture-preparation-second approach.

I know this sounds ludicrous, but this is actually what I did do in the Winter quarter. For the balance of the Fall (and for most of the rest of the year, as well), I simply closed my eyes and pretended she wasn't there.

I could and should have assigned Mr. White to an upper division course, but thought him unqualified. He was unqualified, of course, but it would have been better to sacrifice the older students, already ruined at the font of his misinformation, than destroy our entering freshmen. I switched his assignments in the Winter quarter, which precipitated a crisis, but by Winter almost all my decisions seemed to trigger one form of resistance or another.

Ms. Samahapathabana was still with us; her tears had gotten to me or perhaps I was just protecting myself from an error I'd made with her at our first meeting, a natural instinctive gesture: finding her crying, I had given her a brief hug. I am a hugger by nature, but hugs are out today, even, they tell me, even between parents and children. Rather than have this particular hug misconstrued, and perhaps my hands did touch her breasts, which, unusually large for an Asian, were difficult to avoid, I kept Ms. S on the faculty. I planned (unsuccessfully as it turned out) to keep my hands well off her, then free the department of her in the year following. But for the moment, she was on the staff and had to be given students to teach (students who, after a few weeks of not hearing and not heeding her tiny voice, would ignore her, would learn nothing, would be a burden to future instructors but would—the up side I suppose—not complain).

Dean Holley congratulated me (by telephone) on the new people I had hired, and inwardly I congratulated myself <grin> on having a man like the Dean for a boss. My congratulations were premature.

My Dean may have been a superb educator prior to his first retirement, one of the few who still recognized merit, but he could not or would not do anything about the department's problems.

A nod of assent from my Dean meant only that I had permission to raise my concerns with a higher authority. If the higher authority, Beau-Beau Lee, concurred, then the Dean would affix his signature. If the higher authority took exception—Beau-Beau's most common response—then it was my neck on the chopping block.

In addition to the 1001 duties of my new position:

the too-many, too-frequent meetings—with the Dean (individually and as part of a group of his department heads), with my own faculty (group plus one-on-one sessions), with the faculty senate, with the senate steering committee, the university committee on the arts (I like music), and the computer advisory committee (total ignorance here);

the need to rewrite syllabuses and course descriptions, and to maintain two academic programs—one for our advanced students who desperately needed the training they should have, but hadn't received as freshmen and sophomores, and one for our beginning students for whom (initially) hope still existed;

marketing these programs (at the time I took over as department head, the vast majority of neighboring health-related institutions, dental schools, optometric colleges, and so forth, had more or less given up on Benjamin);

marketing our students (ditto for all the employers in the area who rated a Benjamin College degree only marginally better than a high-school equivalency certificate);

marketing to new students (trying to attract a better class of student by convincing them that, yes, Benjamin was a better place to get a prehealth degree);

my job was to teach, five days a week, two to three hours each day.

I taught anatomy and was immensely pleased to look down that first morning on a classroom packed with students, each of whom had obviously signed up to take advantage of the better quality of education my presence offered.

My pleasure diminished at two p.m. that same afternoon when I counted only one student (1) in the anatomy laboratory. This individual, a short, jug-eared male was, anomaly of anomalies, a Caucasian. "Where is everybody?" I asked jocularly.

"Oh, you don't have to take the laboratory;" he replied, "I just thought a lab would help me to get into medical school."

"You don't have to take the lab!" I repeated in a voice that came close to a scream. (It was clear now I would have to go back on my blood pressure medication.) "You have to take the lab. Every anatomy student has to take a lab." Yes, I definitely was screaming.

My solitary student—more and more his bent posture reminded me of Kermit the frog—shrugged. And he had a right to shrug; it wasn't his problem; he was present prepared to take the lab; the other students weren't. So I shut down my whining and lectured, as much as one does in a laboratory, briefly and to the point—"the skeleton is divided into two main groupings—the axial and the appendicular. The axial skeleton, in turn, may be subdivided into the skull, the vertebral column and the bony thorax. The skull, which we will examine today, may be grouped into two sets of bones, the cranium which consists of eight large flat bones, and the face which consists of fourteen. Altogether, we have 206 bones whose names and features we must learn. By subdividing them into groups, we reduce the problem to a series of simple easily-definable tasks." So saying, I thrust a skull and a lab manual into Kermie's hands and beat it out the door.

I was in the Dean's inner office within five minutes. Surprisingly, he was there also, although he was on the telephone and I had to wait while he negotiated rates with a dishwasher repairman. The Dean let me blow off steam, then asked, plaintively, if we couldn't put these changes off until next semester. "No," I puffed, "whoever heard of an anatomy course without an anatomy lab!"

"Your predecessor," the Dean remarked acidly. "I'll take your word for it that the changes are necessary, but before I can authorize them, we need to be sure there are no conflicts."

"Conflicts?" I was screaming inwardly again but then I have a natural paranoia that stands me well in most human contacts.

"With schedules, with course descriptions, and, for all I know, with University policy. Talk to the Registrar, the Dean of Students, and

Beau-Beau, of course." The Dean smiled toothily much as the Wizard of Oz must have done when he asked Dorothy to bring back the broomstick of the Wicked Witch of the East.

Fortunately, all three of the above-named personalities were willing to see me that afternoon, even if, to a person, their approval was contingent on that of the next individual in the chain. I knocked on doors, waited in outer offices, smiled when I felt like scowling. My efforts (and my inward agony) paid off: three times around, including two additional visits to my Dean, and I'd established a record for Benjamin College: a change had been effected (subject, of course, to the approval of the full Academic Senate). The Dean shook his head when he heard about my progress. "Sometimes it's best not to be too successful," he cautioned.

The students were not pleased. Thirty sullen black faces recoiled in horror the next morning when I told them they must register for the laboratory. "I can't." "How'm I goin' get money?" "The bookstore don't have any manuals." "We's no time to sign up for the course."

I solved the time problem by letting the students out fifteen minutes early. The missing lab manuals were more difficult: "The students hardly evah takes de lab," the bookstore lady told me, but she agreed to place a rush order (though she delayed phoning it in till the following day) and Mz. Washington the bottle-dyed, tawny-haired departmental secretary helped me with copying the first

Chapters of the manual by showing me where the copying machine was.

Recoiling at the prospect of doing the copying myself—who was the secretary here and who was the boss—and having recalled seeing my secretary deep in conversation with a young student when I walked into the departmental office, I ventured, "Perhaps that student might help me?"

Mz. W's answer verified my worst suspicions. "De worker?" she asked.

"Yes. Could she do this copying for me?"

"Oh, she much too busy."

By two p.m. the next afternoon, I had printed out thirty copies of the

Chapter on bones, more than enough for the fifteen students who actually appeared for the laboratory.

"A fifty percent drop in enrollment is not a good sign," said the Dean to me in our private over-the-telephone after-meeting meeting the following week.

"But President Benjamin always says he's looking for better students, not more students."

"Yes, that's all very well for the President, but we have financial realities to consider. Your salary for instance."

I gasped, incredulous.

"That's just an example; obviously, your particular salary comes out of a special fund. But in general, when we lose students, we lose faculty, also. Just take it as a given, that while we do want better students, we want to retain the existing students as well."

"A nod is as good as a wink to a blind horse," I said, though I'd no idea at all what I was talking about.

My faculty was equally grave when we met that week; for once even Mrs. Black and Mr. White put in an appearance. I could hear them all, even those who owed their jobs specifically to me, whispering about declining enrollments and layoffs before the meeting began.

The meeting was not a success. Mrs. Black and Mr. White were on the attack while my allies were remarkably silent. Only Miss Samahapathabana attempted a justification, but few were able to hear or understand her.

Afterwards I tried to thank her, and when she again looked as if she were about to cry, I put an arm around her, a gesture, I'm afraid, that only created another opportunity for misinterpretation of my motives.

Miss S always looked so grateful for any attention. Apart from our tear-filled after-meeting encounters, in subsequent weeks, I often found myself bringing her little gifts of candy. A day or so later, she would appear at the door of my office near lunch time with a gift of some spicy Thai dish for the two of us to share behind closed doors.

The pattern was set and it was just a question of when, not whether, it would go amiss.

"What you and Miss S up to?" Miz Washington asked me one day. It was Miz Washington who had the happy idea of calling Miss S, Miss S.

"Lunch," was my terse reply.

If only I could have penetrated Miss Samahapathabana's accent and found out what her true dreams and desires were. If only our students, likewise could have made sense of her fevered intelligence. We met for lunch, I brought her head down into my lap and she sucked me dry.

"It's been a hell of a day," I said to Peri.

"You want to go to the play," was her only reply to my fevered plea for pity and understanding. I looked puzzled and, I hoped, weary, but it did not abate her enthusiasm. "The High School is doing 'Once Upon a Mattress.'"

I choked back a half dozen obvious snotty replies—I'd seen Mattress with Carol Burnett in the title role, the only saving grace for this least memorable of musicals, and still loathed it thoroughly. A good thing I did restrain myself, for Peri added, "My nephew's in it."

"Then let's see it," I replied matching her enthusiasm. Having three daughters of my own, I willingly suspend disbelief when children are involved. A bad musical badly done can be wonderful fun when the nephew of the one you love is in it. As It turned out, her nephew wasn't in it really—he did something or other back stage and she wasn't sure just what till after the performance.

A lot of people said hello to me in the auditorium, either because I'd done business with them—like the Korean who owned the dry cleaners, or because they taught at Benjamin—I wasn't alone in seeking the comforts of Pineville, or because they knew Peri and felt that because they knew Peri, they knew me. A lot of half-cousins, all identical towheads though of varying shapes and sizes, fell into this category and I loved them all because I loved this small delicate creature who sat by my side enraptured by the familiar play.

Have I said I know it all? It's one of my problems. I've got degrees in both mathematics and anatomy, sang in the university choir, was the stage manager once for the Orestia and played God in J.B. I think I know how musicals are to be staged. But none of this knowledge meant as much to me as the changing expressions on Peri's face. Like a child, I thought for an instant, and then sat up sharply in my chair. Peri wasn't a child; she must have had a life of her own and someone else she'd shared it with before me. Where had she lived before she came to Pineville? what had she done?

"We've never talked about your previous life." I said to her.

"What?" she replied, distracted.

"Where you've been, what you did before I met you."

"Shh." She said. "I love this song. That's Harold Burch." I shook my head, wondering whom she was talking about. "Mz. Burch' son. Joanne, the woman I work for."

"Shh," said others in the seats around us, and this ended the discussion.

The kids at the high school took two curtain calls. We got home quite late, had sex, and I never got to say, "Help me Peri, it's all falling apart."

I dreamed harsh dreams, lie half awake from two a.m. to four participating in imaginary meetings and lecturing before shades in imaginary classes. And the next day, my work began all over again.

(Yet sometimes, now, I wake in the morning still wondering who Peri is, who I am, not worried about losing her, but about finding her every day by my side. Is this the woman I shall choose to marry? Each time I get a call from one of my daughters I ask myself, is Peri the woman my wife was? Am I a better man?)

Chapter 8.

Peri is a wonderful woman; the knowledge grows on me each day we sleep together. Not just because of the sex, which, all consuming, relaxes and rebuilds me, or her cooking, equally an expression of love, but for her common-sense approach to so many of life's problems.

The time will come when we can share an outlook, will have confronted and overcome some crisis together, are able to act and think as a couple. Not now, perhaps, but later.

Her only one unsatisfactory trait in my eyes is an adamant refusal to listen or get involved in my work. Oh, she'll hear me out on occasion, perhaps make a suggestion on how to get this or that individual motivated, but "I just don't want to hear about that college," she will say in the end, shuddering, and I am left to wonder whether it is the black students and faculty, or Benjamin's notoriously poor academic reputation, or simply the notion of an institution, any institution, that sets her off.

Chapter 9.

"Meet the Presnident" read the engraved invitation from the College," which went on to describe an unparalleled opportunity to shake the hand of Benjamin's President the following Tuesday in the college gymnasium, followed by a half hour or so of inane conversation with one's colleagues while munching bread and cheese and whatever else might be snatched from the potluck table.

I didn't need (or much care) to meet the "Presnident." I'd met him at my initial interview, all warmth and ingratiating friendliness, and then been snubbed by him half a dozen times since.

I'm not sure what I expected from President Benjamin—regular debriefing sessions at which he and I would plan strategy for the entire college—but some slight recognition of my existence would have been nice. Though we often sat next to one another at meetings, apart from my once being asked to fetch a chair, we'd not even exchanged "hellos."

Still, I left the invitation out on the telephone table where Peri would be sure to see it. It would be fun to go with her to the college, to show her off and show her around.

"You've got to go," Merrill said to me. (Merrill was very big on formalities.) "It's expected of you, part of your job."

"Merrill says it's expected of me," I repeated to Peri that night at dinner.

"What will you wear?" she countered.

I offered a choice of jackets and she said she'd check my clothing over. She didn't say she'd be going with me, though.

"The reception will be a good chance for you to meet Nelson," Merrill observed, when we met the next day at lunch. Now, I had to go.

The big man on the Benjamin campus was not me, as I may have led you to suppose, but Nelson Ellis in the English Department.

My Dean said, "Oh yes, him," when I brought up Ellis' name, but I knew who Nelson was all right. I had all his books, dog-eared, in the collection I carry with me from job to job.

If you're not already a fan, you may still remember *Code-Name Madeline,* the book of Nelson's that almost made the best-seller list—

it had a large cult following, at least in Berkeley. In *Madeline*, Nelson mixes the present and the past: the girl he is dating is the present; her aunt Madeline, a heroine in the French underground during World War II, the past. Although the niece is a warm, living presence in his arms, it is the aunt, dead and utterly beyond reach, who most attracts him. I thought the book was great. Who did the author really care for? The girl or her aunt, somewhere in time?

I wanted to talk about *Madeline* and *I Love You Maggie* (another favorite of mine) with Mr. (Dr.?) Ellis or, better, to find out about his next book—a new one hadn't appeared in almost a decade—but Nelson didn't seem to talk to anyone. He skipped faculty meetings and I'd never seen him in conversation with any of the people I knew on campus.

So I left the invitation on the phone table, and made a point each evening at dinner of talking with Peri about how much fun the reception promised to be.

By the night of the reception, she still hadn't committed herself. I knew she didn't have an excuse. She'd already told me her aerobics class had been canceled. "Great, you can come with me. I'll wait while you change."

She shook her head. Her lips were pursed; her expression set in unchangeable lines. My immovable angel, blond hair back lit by the fading light from the window, pale skin fresh and cherubic. And, despite my willingness to recite these and other compliments, completely unwilling to come with me.

She did not care for the place where I worked. O.K. Someday, maybe, she would tell me why. Stuffing a paperback copy of *I Love You Maggie* into my jacket pocket—my sole remaining copy of *Madeline*, a hardbound edition, was just too heavy to lug around—I went out the door to my car.

The Benjamin College gymnasium was packed with sweating, perfumed guests: Faculty, students, administrators, the Fort Lee Chamber of Commerce, dignitaries and distinguished alumni from as far away as Atlanta. Just walking across the gym from the door to the food tables was a workout, and the reception line promised an hour-long wait.

Academia's lower orders—custodians, clerks, and secretaries, were also much in evidence. Our campus leaders, only a generation removed from a sharecropper/servant background, would not turn their backs on those who'd sired them. I'd no trouble encountering people I didn't want to meet—Miss S, in particular, seemed determined to take the place of the absent Peri by my side—but I'd come there to network, to brown nose with senior administrators and, above all, to get Nelson Ellis' signature on my copy of *I Love You Maggie*.

Mrs. Angel stood in back of the food tables looking careworn and browbeaten, but still incredibly attractive. Normally, she was a fleeting figure, a ship's prow, glimpsed by me at most once a day, walking to the cafeteria or as we came and went from our cars. Now seemed my chance to enlarge on our acquaintance.

Her eyes, though, were riveted on the far end of the gymnasium where a group of senior administrators surrounded the President. Next to them, her husband, Al Angel, the Dean of Agriculture, stood among a laughing circle, his right hand cupping the elbow of an attractive but overweight black woman.

I'd sat on a number of committees with Al. A large man, broad-shouldered and barrel-chested, he was jovial when he got his way, domineering and physically intimidating when he didn't. I wasn't quite sure I liked him. Though black as the blackest man on campus, he'd had his pick of the white fraternities at Ohio State, and, judging by Mrs. Angel, of the women in the nearby white sororities.

A short white man with horn-rimmed glasses stood next to him. Nelson Ellis! It had to be. I stepped forward, only to find my arm gripped tightly and Mrs. Angel's warm voice in my ear.

"Dr. Wood, I'd like you to meet these two lovely ladies."

The two white women who stood next to Mrs. Angel at the refreshment table did not have a fraction of her glamour or her poise. They simpered during the introductions, even giggled as Mrs. Angel and I exchanged glances. Shy, almost diffident, marginally self-confident with me, they whispered in the presence of the other guests, mainly blacks, who hovered around the service table.

Waitresses, I thought. White waitresses at a black party. Why did Mrs. Angel introduce me to them?

The stout white woman who came out of nowhere to pump my hand was an entirely different type. "I'm Ruth Thompson," she said, "Home Economics. I hear you were at Berkeley."

"Mmm," I replied, noncommittal, my attention now divided four ways among Nelson—where had he gone?—Mrs. Angel, the two Mrs. Whatsits, and this new person.

Mrs. Thompson proceeded to tell me she'd been a faculty member at the University of Wisconsin—I was suitably impressed—and that she knew two or three people I might have known at Berkeley—I didn't know any of them. Her account was punctuated by frequent nervous laughter and this laugh and the din around us may have been the reasons I didn't completely catch her explanation of why she was no longer at Wisconsin.

"I really wasn't responsible for what happened," she concluded, leaving me wondering, but too polite to ask. Had she poisoned the college Dean with her Tomato Surprise or set fire to Wisconsin's test kitchens?

"It was good meeting you," I temporized, resolving never to eat anything prepared by Mrs. Thompson's hand, and set out again in search of Ellis.

Ms. S had been lurking close by. "Hi," she said shyly, or at least this is what I thought she said; as always, her voice was on the near edge of audibility. "I want to see you." I heard her say that, clearly, and immediately was afraid we'd been overheard by one of the many people around us.

"Mrs. Thompson. This is Ms. Samahapathabana." I pronounced each syllable of the long Thai name. "She is a wonderful cook," I added, leaving the identity of "she' to be resolved between them.

The two women looked at each other without interest. The three of us stood together for a few moments without speaking, an oasis of silence, while I cast about for a plausible excuse to leave them.

An older white woman with a mannish hairstyle and narrow hips tapped me on the shoulder. "You're Peter, aren't you?" she said, addressing me by my given name. "I've heard so much about you."

Yes? And who the hell are you? "I suppose you're a colleague of Merrill's," I said aloud.

"Good heavens, no." She laughed, a deep throaty laugh that conveyed genuine warmth. "I'm not one of you genius types. Just an ordinary gym teacher. Oh, and I carry the first-aid kit when our teams go on the road."

Her laughter and easygoing manner were infectious. I smiled and thought about what I might say in reply. "I've always liked jocks," I said.

"Too bad you're taken, then." Her statement should have clued me in to who she was. But how did she know me? Or know that I might be taken? A wide grin took over her features. I felt as if I were being sized up for something, but if not romance, what? "Perhaps we ought to circulate." I suggested.

"You mean we ought to get out of here," she replied derisively, "this place is a zoo." She led me passed one of the two Mrs. Whatsits and out through the temporary kitchen. Drinks in hand, we plodded up a narrow flight of stairs and emerged on the running track that circled the gymnasium.

The noise and confusion appeared to have halted at the track's edge, a trick of the gym's acoustics. "Better." she said from behind me. "Jewel's my name. I grabbed us each a sandwich on the way. You want one? I see you've already got a drink."

I took the crustless sandwich gratefully, then gave Jewel the long steady look I always give a person of the sex of my choice. She didn't seem at all disconcerted. Instead, she looked back with an equally steady gaze, that same unremitting friendliness.

"Like it up here?" she asked. "I've seen you running noontimes."

"You're the aerobics teacher," I exclaimed, placing her for the first time. On those few days when I was able to make time for my noon run around the indoor track in the gym, a dozen or so plump black girls in shorts would be jumping about to music on the floor below, with Jewel standing on a box at their head.

Jewel put her hands on her hips and gave me that once-over look again. "You don't know how I know you, do you."

I blushed my confusion and took too big a sip of my Cuba Libra.

"I'm Peri's aerobic instructor. I teach in Pineville in the evenings and she's told me all about you."

"I wish she were here," I said, truthfully, and glanced down over the railing and away from Jewel unwilling to share too many of my feelings.

What I saw below resembled nothing so much as a mob scene in a silent movie. An occasional black face would look up, mouth open like a goldfish in a bowl, but no sound would emerge.

The room appeared to be divided in layers like a large chocolate cake. "Why are all the black people at one end of the room and the brown people at the other?"

Jewel pressed up beside me next to the rail, though the physical contact lacked any sort of sexual spark. "Mud Pie, right," she said, "thin sprinkling of coconut down by the food tables where Mrs. Angel and the two Mrs. Whatsit's are standing."

"The waitresses?"

"They're not waitresses, they're wives. They're also on the faculty, smart people like yourself, though maybe not quite so smart. One's in English; one's in French. Women folk don't rate very high on the scale down here, and us white women folk are the lowest."

Her accent was mocking, its drawling Southern overtones deliberately accentuated.

"I was thinking more along the lines of chocolate cake." I said, pursing my original thought. "With raisins," I added, noticing the very black Professor Boouressa sticking out amid the rest of my polyglot department, pale white and pale brown that had established themselves by the front doors of the gym.

"Where's Nelson?" I asked. "Nelson Ellis, do you know him?"

Jewel peered over the railing. "Why do you want to meet him?"

"Aren't that many of us white guys here tonight," I said. I liked Jewel, but I couldn't picture her with a copy of *Code Name Madeline*.

"He's not white. Half, maybe. They say he's a son of Lena Horne. She had almost eleven children and about the same number of partners."

I turned and gave Jewel a second look. Eyes like bright pennies. An air of unremitting calm, of content with a world that provided her with an endless source of amusement.

"He wrote some book about his mother, only, to disguise her identity, he set it during the Second World War. He's supposed to talk about having sex with her in the book.

"They say it's all symbolic. Too deep for me." Jewel grinned. "The heroine is really his mother, Lena, and the girlfriend is really her, also."

This explanation was something I did not want to hear, especially coming from someone who taught aerobics and basketball. Why had she attached herself to me in the first place?

"I think I'm going to go back downstairs."

"Suit yourself. But he may not want to meet you because you're white. He thinks of himself as black. You watch. All the people he associates with are black, and much darker than he is. He'll never be caught talking with one of us for fear of being thought one of us."

Right. Intolerant intellectual pretension. Bullshit in other words.

O.K. I was upset because I had my own vision of Nelson's book, a vision I'd clung to for too many years to see it vanish over a Cuba Libra. I had to see him.

Trying not to seem completely rude, I hurried down the stairs and back into the gym. Mrs. Angel was standing against the wall where I'd left her, still staring out at the crowd toward her husband. He was in more or less the same position, only the girl reclining against him was different.

(Why torture yourself. If you know what to expect, then look away.)

Nelson was no longer at Al Angel's side and finding him was going to be far from easy. The crowd was in constant motion, and Nelson, shorter than average, was hidden in the press of bodies.

If the gymnasium were a large clock, then Nelson Ellis had been located at about eight minutes to twelve when I last saw him. Cocktail parties and receptions circulate clockwise—I'd read that somewhere—I would probably do best to head toward noon, the basketball hoop, in search of him.

A moment's walk brought me eye to eye with a familiar face. "President Benjamin," I said, but he merely grunted in return. The reception line ended, he'd been reduced to waiting on the fringes of a circle that had formed about several of the visiting dignitaries. Talking in a calm authoritative voice to one of Houston County's black legislators was a tall, balding mulatto whom I vaguely recognize. I saw my Dean also. He smiled at me and essayed a wave, but I knew better than to follow up on it.

Unthinkingly, I backed into a large black man behind me. Al Angel took the collision calmly and helped me to regain my balance. "Professor Wood," he said, all teeth, "You goin' to do some good work for us?"

Al was standing with one arm around the waist of a tawny brown woman who might easily have passed for an exotic dancer, though her true role was in accounting. Our head librarian and the evil Mrs. Black were also part of Al's current entourage, the look in their eyes suggesting they were just waiting their own turn to lean back on his arm.

Al put one large hand down on my shoulder and gave it a friendly squeeze. Nodding toward Mrs. Black, he said in a put-on Southern accent, "Now don't you go giving my frien' too hard a time. She jus' tryin', same as the rest of us."

Right, I thought, and smiled weakly, resisting the impulse to rub my shoulder where he'd squeezed it.

"I'm looking for Nelson Ellis," I said.

"He aroun',"' Mrs. Black replied, and all four blacks gave me a look which said as clearly as if we'd been standing on the edge of an Atlanta slum, "move on Whitey."

I looked here; I looked there. I circulated around the upper part of the gymnasium twice and once even penetrated the lower part near the double doors, where the lesser fry stood drinking pop. Miss S's eyes lit on me each round—she looked more and more disconsolate—and I knew I would have to make up my neglect to her the following day.

The crowd grew thinner—I still had not found Nelson—and finally my only choice was to acknowledge Ms. S. or to leave. I left.

Outside, the chill night air provided the first indication that Georgia's prolonged summer had given way to fall. Eyes on the stars, I found myself in an unfamiliar and almost deserted parking lot.

"Lost," a warm woman's voice called out to me.

Jewel again. "I never found him," I confided, meaning Nelson.

She grinned, but could as easily have said, "I told you so."

"I'll walk." I said, when she asked if she could give me a lift to my car. "It's a beautiful night."

The stars that for so long had been lost in the haze of summer stood out now like sparkling diamonds. For a moment, Jewel and I watched them silently and together.

"You be good to her," she said, rolling up her window, and drove out of the lot, still grinning.

I knew she meant Peri. I thought of the questions I'd wanted to ask Jewel all evening. "How did you know who I was? How'd you know so much about Peri and I? What made you stop and talk to me?" But she was already gone.

Chapter 10.

7:40 AM. Thirty or forty minutes of peace before I must be on the road to campus. I can go back to bed, have another cup of coffee, or simply sit here and try to fit together what has become of my life.

My relationship with Peri came too easily. The sex is great—everything just as I might have fantasized—but we slipped into intimacy too quickly, skipped all the intervening steps.

Who is this person who lies next to me at night? Who kisses me, one hand on my shoulder, one hand caressing the back of my neck, says "I love you" each morning before she slips out the door on the way to work? I move about her cottage with care, taking the extra pains I should have taken with my wife: coffee cup and plates rinsed and put away in the dishwasher, cupboards closed after opening, toilet seat down. I do it not out of love, but deliberate habit; it's got to go right this time, I think.

Things at work are falling apart, not at all what I expected. Faculty and students are inches from open revolt. With my daughters and my ex three thousand miles away, my relationship with Peri is all I have.

I'm not sure yet what it is I am preserving or who it is I am living with. Have I ever before questioned the nature of the woman beside me? Impatient to bed, I skip the details, listen only to convince the woman of my sincerity and forget what she said almost the moment she says it. Not in Peri's case. I want to know who she is, how she became that way, (and why she has chosen me). But she is a mystery, as much a mystery as why only whites live in our part of town when family after family of blacks live only a few blocks away. (In the morning, when the children walk to elementary school, the two streams, black and white, merge on the corner where the traffic guard, an elderly white man one day, a young black woman the next, wait to escort the children.)

Peri's ambivalence bothers me. We live only in the now, never discuss our children—I assume she has them—or our past marriages. Though half my life or more is spent on campus and commuting to and from, it is only that minor part of my life in Pineville we share. Merrill has asked me, what, half a dozen times, to come to his home for dinner. "And bring your little lady." Somehow, he has learned of Peri. Who told? The black postman? Or has Merrill other friends and contacts among the whites of Pineville? This latter explanation is the more likely. Perhaps, Peri's family, too, like many in the South, has its other, darker side.

"Bring your little lady."

I can't say she won't come. Instead, I reply that Peri has a class, or must go into work to cover for someone else. (Will Merrill know if she does not go into work? We live in such a small town.) I offer to come alone. He says, no, we'll do it some other time. And so through Peri's intransigence I'm cut off entirely from one part of the Georgia community. (What is life like in the home of a Negro, even one as upper class and respectable as Merrill?)

Peri be my wife. Share my life with me.

Chapter 11

The chemistry laboratory scared the hell out of me.

It bothered me even to visit the room. Its single entrance led to a death trap that held one instructor and eighteen students. On the far wall, a lone fire extinguisher seemed inadequate to cope with any real emergency.

A heavy smell of chemicals pervaded the air even when the lab was not in use, suggesting the ventilation system was inadequate. Cabinets weren't vented separately. Flammables and caustic agents were stored side by side in metal cabinets already rusted from the fumes.

The explosion-proof refrigerator used to store volatile chemicals was located in the biology laboratory next door, only it wasn't explosion proof, just an ordinary refrigerator with a light that went on like a match head when one opened its door.

No safety shower—in case a student splashed chemicals on herself—no eye spray, no signs warning of chemical hazards (either in the lab or anywhere in the building), no fire alarm nor phone near by. I wasn't sure what all the applicable safety regulations were, but I knew we had to be in violation of a great many of them.

I brought up my concerns (though not my fear) at our weekly faculty meeting and found my teaching staff quite supportive; each had their own separate set of horror stories:

A student had splashed acid into his eye—his fault really, we did insist they pay for and wear safety goggles—and was given a waiver to sign before being examined by the school nurse.

A Bunsen burner tipped and an entire bench top set alight like some enormous cherries jubilee before Professor B had the presence of mind to cover the bench with the mat he was standing on. The solitary fire extinguisher, well out of reach, proved empty.

I tried to take Professor B to task for his failure to report these and other deficiencies. He replied he had complained—to my predecessor and my predecessor's predecessor, and that nothing had ever come of it. Dr. Farmer—easily our most popular instructor, provided me with a manual used by the county high schools titled, "Health and Safety Regulations for the School Laboratory." I copied relevant portions and passed them on to my boss the Dean. He agreed (surprise) that change was essential; at his suggestion, I made additional copies and gave them to Beau Beau Lee and to Carver Brown, the Head of Building and Grounds, but received no response from either party.

Their lack of response, of interest, was frustrating, crazy making. I was learning that my boss, the Dean, had three approaches to problems:

The first was to dump the entire mess back in my lap: "You're creative; you'll think of something."

The second was to appeal to my loyalty to the school, "We just haven't got the money, now. I can tell them (meaning Beau Beau Lee, the Vice-President for Academic Affairs, and a Mr. Nathaniel who had something to do with finance) about the problems, but they can't do anything about it until we get through the budgeting process."

"Next month?" I suggested.

"We can give it a try."

It took almost all of my first semester before I realized that 'next month' was the Dean's third and final solution.

Beau-Beau Lee, the Vice President for Academic Affairs was more candid when I raised the issue of the chemistry laboratory. "We hired you to take care of problems like this."

I thought over what he'd said, and though his tone suggested he was not prepared to debate this or any other issue, ventured that we might be laying ourselves open to a law suit, "if there is an accident, that is."

The next day the Dean was all over me. "I thought you were a team player," he said. "I thought you and I were working together to solve these problems."

"Yes, but you sounded like you wouldn't be able to do much to help me."

The Dean covered his face with his hands. "You just don't understand." I started to reply, but he shushed me. "Peter. May I call you Peter? You're bright, no question about it, very bright; you're hard-working, you've got a lot of good ideas, and the department has made a lot of progress under your leadership. I, personally, am amazed at how fast and how far we've come. But Peter, sometimes we're not the only one who has ideas. You've got to learn to give the other fellow credit, to try to see things from the other fellow's point of view."

I didn't understand. My experience told me if a problem exists, fix it. But as far as my Dean was concerned, I and not the chemistry laboratory was the problem.

"They just don't care," I said to Professor B and he gave me a comradely nod of understanding.

I wanted, needed Peri's input. Peri had suggested the gift of a tape of Persian music for the homesick Dr. Amani. He'd loved the tape, had repaid the gift a hundred times with loyalty and little gifts of food. Peri had advised me to befriend Carver Brown, Head of Building and Grounds, and to call again on Mrs. Angel who, it proved, was charged with tracking vacant offices. Peri would probably have had a solution for this latest crisis.

Unfortunately, when I needed Peri most, she could not be there to help me. In spirit, perhaps, but her body had been taken hold of by a fever. For three days, I kept her full of Tylenol, wrapped up tightly in an Afghan during the day and close to the warmth of my own body at night. I made her drink fluids until she grew to hate me—"Now, I've got to go to the bathroom because of you," she kept saying.

She got better of course, but when I didn't get the flu in turn, she accused me of having given it to her in the first place. (Well, maybe I did bring the flu home from school; certainly, the college was regularly taken over by epidemics of sickness: flu, mononucleosis, and once even three cases of measles that I'd thought an extinct disease.) Her accusation only emphasized what I'd feared from the beginning: how very different Peri and I were, how tenuous our relationship.

Without her guidance, I soldiered on. I made some changes in the teaching assignments for the winter quarter—on paper; I wasn't sure how much change I could enforce when push came to shove. I put down Mr. White for an extra laboratory and switched Professor B to freshman classes.

I began cleaning up. A set of unlabeled bottles were the first to go, followed (almost) by a host of outdated chemicals, acids that had been left unstoppered, metals that had been improperly wrapped.

The "almost" was occasioned by the sudden discovery that the school had never bothered to obtain a disposal permit.

When I reported this deficiency via the usual chain of command, it was suggested I might "sneak" the chemicals out of my lab or pour them down the drain. I compromised and asked Building and Grounds to pick up the overflowing canister of liquid wastes. (Let them take the heat.) Meetings were held—I wasn't invited—the very next week, a solution arrived: a second empty canister placed side by side with the overflowing first.

Oh, and on the last day of the Fall term, Professor Raffield of Agriculture Science showed up demanding to know where his bottles were. His Dean, Al Angel, had a lot to say to my Dean, but. . . never mind.

Chapter 12.

We lie next to each other, Peri's small breast cupped in my hand. She has taken to placing her own hand around my testicles while we sleep.

Our relationship has gone far beyond what I planned originally. She is an important person in my life; in my leisure moments, few these days because of the complexity of my job, I think of her as my only source of peace and satisfaction.

Why do I stay with her? We do not have that much in common. She has gone with me to Atlanta, more or less willingly to see the Alvin Ailey Dancers—she "liked it, sorta;" (actually, I didn't care for them myself that much, would have preferred something more Agnes de Mille; "Agnes de Mille?"), and the Dave Murray Octet (absolutely wonderful; the group has the greatest trombone player in the world;)—she didn't care for them: "Too many blacks," and "I don't like it when they play all by themselves like that, I thought it would be more like a band."

She wouldn't go to any of the events I went to at Benjamin such as the Faculty Jazz Concert. (Very few Benjamin students went to this concert either. Nobody told them blacks were into jazz, nor would they have cared. They were into hip-hop and rap and whatever music set them apart from all the other generations before them.)

I wanted to go to cult films (which would have necessitated a trip to Atlanta); Peri just wanted to see a movie, and any movie would do.

She read books, but did not acquire them the way I do, by buying them at a bookstore or going to the library; she brought them home from her job, appropriated or loaned or simply forgotten by someone she worked with.

She knew who Steven King was, but not Steven Bachman. She didn't know the MacDonald's (John D., Ross, or Harris) and wasn't any more familiar with Sue Grafton or Judith Guest.

I rediscovered Pynchon and Bellow in the college library, read and reread everything they'd written; she tolerated their presence.

It cannot be just the sex that binds us together. Miss S will give me all the sex I need and there is always the possibility that Mrs. Angel or Miss Feret will make herself available. I stay because Peri is more than sex, she is the wind and rain and sun and the point of my existence. I give to her and feel, yes, I, too, am important.

She is not beautiful; well, yes she is, though not in a Barbie-like way. The sun and wind have worn lines in her face, rivulets in the red Georgia clay; but her eyes are fresh and clear as a child's and sparkle with an inner light. She is youthful and mature, fairylike, sedate.

We walk together in the park, along the paths that wind among the ball diamonds, sometimes by chance at the end of a warm afternoon, watching the growing shadows bring the cool of evening, sometimes by choice, when driven by the need to unwind, I try to walk off the frustration of another wearying day.

We both have a favorite place, a small copes of woods at the park's boundary, with a creek bed at its foot. The creek is dry except for a short period after each storm, when it rushes and gurgles in tune with the rain. We like the smell of the gum trees and the crushed leaves. Frequently, if no other persons are in sight, we will stop here and kiss, and then walk back to our home.

Once, we glimpsed another couple through the trees. Both the boy and the girl could have been no more than 13 or 14. But the girl was white and the boy was black. "Is that an integrated couple, we saw?" I asked Peri, teasing.

"We didn't see anything," she replied vehemently.

Chapter 13.

The headline in the evening paper said a Benjamin student had been found dead in the college swimming pool that morning. He was found by a custodian floating in the pool or else face up on the pool's bottom. The newspaper, printed in Pineville, actually provided both descriptions without any attempt to reconcile or comment on the discrepancy.

Peri showed me the article as we sat side by side on the couch after dinner that evening. I was embarrassed, if for no other reason then I'd been on campus all day and hadn't heard a word about the death.

"You're just too wrapped up in your work."

But surely I'd talked to half a dozen people outside of my department: Merrill, of course, the woman who ran the bookstore and her assistant, a couple of professors in the music department who'd sat next to me at lunch. Not one of them had said anything to me about the boy.

The next day was nothing but a series of meetings. Who was responsible for the death? Or, more accurately, who did we as administrators have to show was not responsible?

I couldn't contribute much to the discussion, nor was I really expected to, though I did use the opportunity to suggest that the chemistry laboratory with its overcrowded conditions and lack of emergency exits might also represent a potential source of liability for the College.

The group did not seem inclined to look forward, which may suggest how we came to get ourselves (and that poor student and his family) into such a mess in the first place. We decided to close down the Natorium until further notice (lock the barn door after the horse was stolen) but no one discussed how the facility might be made safer or whether a lifeguard would be appropriate.

It may seem surprising to the reader, but never once did I think to question how that poor unfortunate student came to die. Somehow, for the meeting was as sparse on details of the death as it was on future preventive measures, I came to convince myself it must have happened while he was swimming alone, diving perhaps, or else that he'd been with a group who'd simply walked off without making sure all their buddies were with them.

Peri took me to task that evening for my lack of curiosity. "But didn't you ask?" she persisted.

"I assumed," was my foolish reply.

These meetings were the beginning of my formal disillusionment with the University. (On an informal level, my disillusionment must have begun the day of my arrival. I was still awaiting a permanent office assignment, for example.) Here I was, cheek by jowl with the College's top administrators—the President, the Vice-President for Academic Affairs, the Comptroller, a flock of Deans and Associate Deans and not one seemed to offer or possess the slightest particle of initiative or responsibility.

Pleased at first at being invited to participate, by the end of the day, I was puzzled by why I'd been summoned at all. No one solicited or even cared for my opinion. I moved my lips to smile, my head to nod approval. (In retrospect, the reason for my inclusion is all too obvious: By bringing in his subordinates, my Dean effectively isolates himself from any and all responsibility. He survives doesn't he? Who am I to question the tactics of a survivor?)

My own plate was not entirely empty. Our one white female student, a Mrs. Elizabeth Mursch, came to me with a complaint of sexual harassment.

Despite what I'd allowed my daughter to infer about ours being an all-black campus, we had two white students: one male, a brilliant young man distorted by premature arthritis, whom I introduced you to in an earlier

Chapter—the drive to Murphysboro and its all-white campus would have meant a daily agony for him; and Becky Mursch, our sole white female student, the wife of a corporal at the nearby air base, who also found our black campus less threatening than the long drive to the whites-only branch of the state university. She, alas, was not as gifted as Kermie, the male, quite the contrary, to the point where I thought of advising her she might be better off in searching for self-fulfillment elsewhere. Alas, her self-image demanded she go to the College. Or, perhaps, she attended to torment her husband whom, she informed me, did not particularly care for her coming "here" either. (Again the ambiguity: did "here" refer to our all-black campus, or was the mere act of attending an institute of higher education provocation enough?) In any event, she stayed, though her grades were marginal and she complained constantly. (All part, I imagine, of what she viewed as the unending battle between the sexes.)

I am not a male chauvinist. Few men with three daughters and no sons can afford to be. Becky was a truly awful student, slow or unwilling to understand, and her complaint that day set her up no higher in my eyes. The alleged harasser was none other than Professor Boourassa, ancient professor of chemistry, graduate of a Cameroon missionary school, the Sorbonne, and Oxford (England), a rare catch for BC, in my opinion and, if the wool on his head were to be trusted, not a man who would go about pinching a young girl's bottom.

It was not so much a question of my judging the book by its cover, I told the young lady, as to the fact hers was the first such complaint to be lodged against the Professor in the twenty years he'd been with the University.

Of course, at that time, I had no idea whether this latter endorsement was accurate; mine was merely the natural protective response of a true obfuscator. I found out later that while the Professor's record had been clean during the ten (not twenty) years he'd been at Benjamin, he had come to us, a giant step down from his previous employment, because of just such an incident of sexual harassment.

I promised Becky (the natural bureaucrat in me rising to the surface) that I would look into her complaint. I told her I would prefer she allow me to handle it informally for the moment. She told me this was all right with her, too, she didn't really want to make trouble for the Professor, he was a good teacher, but she did want him to stop pinching her, for it made her nervous. "There will be no repetitions," I assured her. And, later, when I spoke to Professor B, though I laughed as I told him of her complaint, agreeing with his denials even before he had a chance to voice them, I again used the phrase, "there will be no repetitions."

Becky made no more complaints regarding Professor B, but this was not the last time she would come to my office. She would even make a complaint of sexual harassment against me in the end, though by that time my total commitment to Peri, my ongoing affair with Miss. S and a brief, very brief encounter with our wretched departmental secretary, would forestall any interest I might have had in that poor girl.

(I'm losing it. I'm losing all vestige of humanity. I care now only for me.)

Chapter 14.

No longer a stranger, the students have begun coming to me, some for advice, some for mercy, some simply to say hello. Faces emerge from the crowd. Some, I recognize because they are in my classes, others, simply because we pass at regular intervals in the corridors.

Martin King is a regular at my office—wherever it happens to be located that week. President of the Benjamin student body, he makes it a point to visit with all his professors and anyone else he thinks might do him a favor some day.

A soft rap on the door precedes his entry; he is tall, amiable, plump and unthreatening. Glasses and a beaming smile light up his moon-like face. He always calls me Professor Wood or Doctor, asks intelligent questions and seems genuinely interested in the answers. Many of the questions concern his future career, "Physicians Assistant." I've talked to him also about working for a drug company, perhaps as a salesman.

Once, I sounded him out on a pet cause of mine, a protest march on the Fort Lee Manufacturing Plant.

"A march?" he echoed, the concept had clearly gone over his head.

"They have over a hundred engineers on their payroll," I said. "Fifty percent are from out of state, and not one black."

"And why would we march?" he asked.

"To demand they hire Benjamin graduates."

"Like in the movies." His face brightens; he has understood. "I dunno," he says, and his tone is no longer hearty, "most don't want to stay in Fort Lee. It's all right, at least while in school, but most wants to work in Atlanta."

"Where do you want to work?" I asked him.

"In Fitzgerald. That's where I grew up," he added in response to my puzzled look.

Fitzgerald, Georgia is a town with two doctors, both of them white. Four years from now, when Martin is a certified Physician's Assistant, maybe one of them will want to hire a black. Maybe. I hope for Martin's sake that one will.

Another regular at my office, at least for a short period in the late fall, is Kitisha Jackson. A shy black girl who excels at her studies, she will go on, I assume, to medical school. But somewhere along the line, through father, uncle, grandfather, preacher, she's had beaten into her (I use the word literally) that desirable young ladies never excel.

Praise devastated her. I found out first hand when midway through the term, I pitted her against the other students in an oral quiz.

"What bone is this?" I ask and hold up a femur. The student, Laverna King, responds correctly. "And what bone does it connect to proximally?" I ask the next student in the row, and so on until only two or three students are left standing waiting to answer. Kitisha, carried away by the excitement, is the only one who remembers or is willing to say "Pubic sympysis" the answer to the final question.

The runner up, Val Haxton, a bear of a man/boy with a smiling handsome face and massive shoulders, looks discomfited, but it is Kitisha who is not in class the next day; I have embarrassed her, I learn indirectly through student channels, and when she returns chastised, defeated, with bent shoulders and not a trace of that shy smile, I found so agreeable, she no longer meets my eye and never again volunteers an answer.

The students come to me not only because they have petitions—or anticipate having them; many of these visits are simply to feel out in advance what my response will be—but because they genuinely long for contact with the outside, with the older, if not wiser world they soon will enter.

The petitions—there had been many more of them before I took over, my Dean tells me—I believe he intends this as a compliment—are a sorry lot.

"I came to the classroom at noon, but Ms. S wasn't there.

"I make 'nother appointment for the next day, but I can't get there 'cause my car broke down.

"And I try to call her, but there wasn't no phone, and there wasn't no one in the office to answer the phone anyway.

"She say she going to take off ten percent for each day we was late. Then she say, she wasn't going to look at it at all, cause it was so late. So I said, give me another chance. But what she did, I didn't have it to give her because my dog ate it."

"What's this all about?" I ask Ms. Feret. She was dressed that day in a ribbed yellow sweater that promised she could remedy any emotional or nutritional deprivation I might ever have suffered.

"I imagine he wants a change in grade."

I pretend I don't care that Ms. Feret doesn't care, "The student doesn't say that's what he wants. He just rambles on about missed appointments, dogs and broken-down cars."

"Turn his petition down then, that's your right. You're the chairperson."

I smile at her, devastatingly I hope, trying to convey my admiration, my respect.

"But make sure you give a reason. In the space here." Ms. Feret reaches passed me with a long brown finger, dark red nail on the yellow page, to indicate where I am to put my initials. My heart skips a beat even as my brain goes into high gear.

"A reason? "Failure to state a cause of action." Does that sound legal enough?"

"Whatever."

I'd hoped she'd be impressed by my legal acumen. Perhaps some other time.

Other student petitions demand far more effort on my part. The case of Janivers deLessy occupied me for almost two weeks. She had missed a midterm—medical reasons she alleged—but it was the second midterm she'd missed and her instructor—Mr. Farmer—was unimpressed. "Have her bring me a note from her doctor," I suggested.

A note was produced subsequently, with the doctor's name and address neatly typed at the top. Couldn't afford the stationery? I checked with information; yes, a Dr. Carver was at that number, the only doctor, in fact, in that small town.

I called Dr. Carver. A rich deep voice, its slight quaver betraying the advancing age of this Howard graduate, asked after his niece, Janivers. The first of her generation to be going on to medical school—he hoped. His chuckle suggested he and I shared in the knowledge that Janivers was a credit to the family. Her sister, not quite as gifted, worked for him in the office. We did *not* discuss Janivers' recent medical emergency.

I rejected the petition and Janivers did not question my action; I'm sure her sister must have told her about the call. I earned her respect, though, and that of many of her friends, simply because I had cared enough to phone. (And whose idea had the phone call been? Peri's, of course.)

A student would allege he'd received an unfair grade, that the requirements had been switched on him without notice. I would investigate, talk with the instructor and with the other students in the class.

Were the course requirements in writing? had they been changed? had the students been duly notified?

The truth generally went against the student who'd complained. We would have a talk, face to face: "You and every other student in Professor B's class knew when the assignment was due; the date and class were spelled out in your syllabus. And you knew the penalty for a late submission." (So speaketh Wood the authoritative, the by-the-book administrator. Was this the Wood that scaled the walls of the Campanile at midnight and drove a motorcycle through the undergraduate library?)

"Yes, but..." the student would begin a hastily thought-out reply in defense of the apparently indefensible, "I thought the rules might have changed."

"Why would you think that?"

"So many changes since you took over. Us students don't know what be happening next."

Uh huh.

But these in-your-face encounters were the exception. The vast majority of my students may have been ill-prepared, clumsy over-under achievers, but they were just waiting for someone to challenge them, to show them how to learn. The brightest among them were able to soak up as much in one lecture as it might take you or I a week to assimilate.

The problem was, just as President Benjamin had said it would be, one of unfamiliarity. These students had never picked up the study skills they needed. They didn't know how to learn, or even that one could learn on their own. When I left high school, several centuries ago, I thought only one book, one opinion existed on each subject. The teacher told you the answers and you wrote them down. These students were just the same as I was when I started college, not knowing how to put it all together, how to put their brains to work.

"I want to read that book you told us about," Martin King said. "Where can I get it? Could's I borrow your copy?"

For Martin, as for so many of our students, the library, where you or I might search for books, is not a learning center, but a place to socialize, to while away the afternoon around a long table with a group of friends pretending to do homework until, if one is lucky, another student comes by who's done the work or found a copy of the answers in the files at his fraternity; then, one can take one's turn copying the assignment and not have to miss more than a few words of the conversation.

I told Peri one day, though she was pretending not to listen, how impressed I was with the students' minds if not their discipline. "You know, these students really are going to go on to medical school and they're going to make damn good doctors, just the way we promise in our brochures."

"If they can get in to medical school," Peri replied, going instantly to the core of our problem. For Benjamin had been producing an inferior product for years, with the results that professional schools automatically discounted even our most moderate claims. A Benjamin degree was a terminal degree, and our graduates went on, at best, to work as salesman in medical supply houses or workers on an assembly line.

What can I do about it? Rant or rave as I might about uncooperative senior administrators, in the end, like a ship's captain who must navigate storm after storm in a rusting, far-from-seaworthy boat, the responsibility is entirely mine.

Like the captain of a ship, I have taken to touring the classrooms in health science each day before I leave, looking in briefly at each group, not interrupting, but recording for future reference everything I see. This act seems to give both students and faculty confidence, the feeling they are cared for. And I do care for them. I want them, want us all to succeed.

I've seen Mrs. Angel again.

She talks to herself—I wonder if she is aware of it—holding animated conversations as she walks, alone, to her car each evening. Once I thought she was talking to me. She was staring right at me, her lips moving, but her eyes were wild and unfocused. I had stepped toward her, thinking she was beckoning to me, but stepped back quickly when I saw those eyes. Her skirt brushed my legs as she rushed past, lips moving in a frenzied conversation with an unseen other, and this—the funny, terrible, impossible thing, I'm sure that at least twice she used my name.

Chapter 15.

The inside of the Pineville High School gymnasium probably wasn't prettier or more fragrant than its equivalent twenty miles away at Benjamin, but its redbrick exterior was a good deal more attractive. Translucent glass squares set at intervals made the interior bright and cheerful during the day. And its red brick, mined and baked locally, seemed to fit the landscape.

Peri's class in aerobics was just one of a series of activities that filled the school after regular classes let out. The Pineville Shriners met here on Tuesday evenings, as had the Bluebirds and Brownies earlier in the day, along with a fly fishing class, (which might come in handy once the drought ended), aerobics, aikido, the town council (a closed session), and several sororities aimed at young women of character and breeding.

Peri's class declared itself at some distance. Their music ricocheted off the walls joining with the chatter from the classrooms, my own footsteps echoing in the hallway, a burst of laughter as I walked past a room filled with aging white males. Michael and Janet Jackson strut once more, while inside the gym, a full ton of overweight womanhood struggles to return to their high-school silhouettes, Peri, my Peri, the one exception.

The class' attention is focused on the front of the room where Jewel Larrson stands on a low padded platform resembling a soapbox. Though I'm the only man present, I'm ignored, totally, so fixed is their concentration; Jewel, whom I'd met at the "Presnident's" reception, waves, smiles, seems exceedingly glad to see me. She looks moderately attractive, for Jewel, in grayish white shorts, Keds, and a white sleeveless top.

The class is almost entirely white, the one exception, an overweight black matron (the wife of an Air force Colonel, I find out later) who's chosen the corner position by the gymnasium doors where I'm standing. Her two children, a very small boy and a girl about kindergarten age, play unsupervised on the mats nearby. (They play quietly, having learned, presumably, not to distract their mother during aerobic worship.)

Peri, alas, is kitty-corner from me at the far end of the gymnasium. Unlike its counterpart at Benjamin, this gym lacks the overhead running track that would have allowed me to sneak around next to her. Separating us for the next half hour will be an excess of waist and thigh, with the possible exception of one tall blond bombshell in form-revealing tights.

I'd come to see just what was the lure that drew my loved one from the house two evenings a week and kept her away, too long, at a time when my own needs were greatest.

I would have preferred to be at home with Peri that evening, too. In the few months since school started, I've grown used to and dependent on her warm calming presence at the end of each turbulent day. Aerobics separates us. On Tuesdays and Thursdays, I have at most an hour with her before she leaves. While she is gone, I grade papers, watch T.V., or stand in the back yard watching the overcast sky. She returns just before bedtime and once, after, slipping in bed beside me where I lie half-in and half-out of an uneasy sleep. Without her, I feel helpless and abandoned, the next day among black strangers, totally alone.

The class did not impress me. Their ever-shifting gyrations—steps in place, backbends, thigh flexions, didn't look a lot like real exercise to me. I did one or two of each undemanding movement to prove my masculinity, before subsiding back on my heels and looking about for something real and challenging to do.

A headstand on the mats, with the smallest of the children, eyes-wide watching, ended abruptly when I collapsed halfway. Above me, a series of long white ropes were tied at just slightly above shoulder height. But before I could get into any real mischief, the music ended. The women in the group, startled, looked as if they'd suddenly awakened from a deep sleep. Jewel, smiling, dismissed them with her hands, and stepping down from her platform began to walk side by side with Peri toward the locker room. The rest of her charges followed slowly, sheepishly, still rubbing the cobwebs from their eyes. Soon I was alone in the gym but for the two black children playing on the mats.

I drifted back along the now-quiet school corridors to the front door of the building. The sun had gone down with just enough twilight to guide me to the well-lit parking lot, where the rows of Volvos, Pontiacs and Caddies waited for their owners.

The black woman was the first to appear from the locker room. Opening the trunk of her gray Cadillac, she dispensed orange cardboard juice cartons to her two children who sucked on them happily. The bombshell blond, still in her tights, came next, followed closely by a group of the fatties, somewhat separate and apart, discussing the bombshell, I suppose.

Five more minutes passed. I stood under a magnolia tree waiting, my hands thrust upward into the long lower branches, filled with an energy that needed to be dissipated, a walk, a run, a swing through the trees.

The blond bombshell waved to the black woman and called out "see you next week Gloria," before she stepped into her blue Volvo. Gloria smiled, stood taller than she'd allowed herself to stand all evening, and stepped proudly into her own vehicle, shooing her children before her.

Which left me by myself at the edge of the parking lot, not quite able to swing from a tree, waiting. The several chattering women stood far enough away that I could hear only a few words of their conversation. They'd mentioned "Benjamin" not once but several times. Were they talking about me or about the college? "Swimming pool," "the poor boy," and "what did they expect?" One of the women looked over toward me, smiling as if acknowledging that I was eavesdropping but that this was perfectly all right, her husband did it all the time. Then they, too, were gone, sealed away in their automobiles.

Ten more minutes, fifteen before Peri emerged from the gym still flushed and radiant from the aerobics. Beside her, Jewel moved in long confident strides. Their voices dropped slightly in deference to my presence but otherwise they continued to chatter as I walked over to them.

"Hi you babe," I said and reaching down, scooped Peri up against me and gave her a loud smacking kiss. She kissed back though less fervently.

Jewel, too, looked pleased by our encounter, smiling at both Peri and me as if taking vicarious pleasure in our happiness. Her manner was as abrupt and abrasive as ever. "How's the agitator?" she said by way of greeting.

"Me," I mimed, pointing to my chest in apparent disbelief.

"Well, you're always shaking things up," Jewel said, "at least that's the word that filters down to me."

"I didn't intend," I began, stammering as I searched for the words, "So much is wrong with the facilities. The risk of a disaster is incredible. We need to protect ourselves and the students."

"Dear." Peri's voice. A single word and then her finger was on my lips shushing me, her breast brushing against my arm, deliberately teasing. "Jewel doesn't want to hear about the lab."

"And you don't either," I accused.

She shook her head, her blond hair curling up at the ends, still slightly damp from the shower. "Leave your work at work. That's what my Daddy always said. It worked well for him and for us kids, too. Leave your work at work."

"Sounds like good advice to me," Jewel said.

And who asked you, I thought. My feelings must have shown, for Jewel added, "There, I've done it again. Put in my two cents where it's not wanted."

Peri bristled and almost slipped from my grasp.

"Well, I want your advice," Peri said, "And I'm glad you're my friend." She put her other arm around Jewel's waist, linking the three of us. Jewel glowed with happiness, her expression much like my own when Peri is near me, much as I felt myself at that moment.

When we got home, and were undressing for bed Peri, said to me, continuing the earlier conversation, "Protect yourself, first. When you're established, then you can worry about others."

She had slipped her blouse over her head by that time. The sight of her naked form aroused me, forestalled further discussion.

Protect myself. Would I ever be established?

Chapter 16.

My Christmas vacation was less pleasant than I'd imagined it would be. On the plus side, I spent two delightful weeks on the West Coast with my daughters, cementing a firm relationship with the oldest, and rebuilding bridges with my two youngest. They'd not taken sides exactly after the divorce, it was more that in their final teenage years they'd developed a plague-on-both-your houses attitude, hating mother and father equally.

But we played together on this visit, just as we had when they were pre-teens—a walk on the beach, trips to Knott's and Disneyland, sneaking in to adults-only night clubs, and we talked and we held each other and we cried. And, still, with all the excitement and the laughter, I missed Peri terribly.

Who was she? By California terms, a nothing and a nobody, white trash from a southern nigger-hating backwoods hollow. But by my own terms, she was tiny hands, warm, loving fingers I felt caress and stroke the hollow of my back even when I was away from her.

"Let's go sledding," Peri said.

I grunted in reply. At the time, one weekend shortly after school had begun again in January, we were staring at less than two inches of snow that barely covered the not-yet-frozen grass.

I'd been hard pressed to make a snowball, though I had collected enough snow to demonstrate my expertise and make Peri call quit. (Later, while pretending to adjust my collar, she put a handful of snow down my back, but this was a dastardly act of treachery that she never could have duplicated in a fair fight.)

We were sitting inside the house, clothes steaming, when she brought up the subject of sledding a second time. Again, I grunted and gave her an incredulous look. Too cold and too wet for a walk, too warm and not enough snow to go tobogganing. A perfect day for grading papers and not much else.

But she'd taken my grunt for assent. Stepping glassy-eyed from my study several hours later, I discovered the car had been packed and sandwiches made; I was told in no uncertain terms to carry myself and any uncorrected papers out to the driveway.

We didn't exactly travel through trackless wastes of snow initially to reach our destination. On the heavily traveled Interstate, the brief scattering of white stuff had largely melted; the road was black and straight as a knife cut through a brick of ice-cream. But when we left the Interstate an hour or so to the north of Atlanta, the snow began to pile up around us, and the air was thicker and thicker with falling flakes.

As we moved up into the hills, entering that section common to Tennessee, Kentucky, Georgia, and North Carolina in the Smoky Mountains, that is not on any map, whose twisting roads are known only to those who live or have lived there, to the ridge runners, to Peri and her family, the pieces of the puzzle began to fall into place: Peri was from these same ridges, was as alien to the fertile bottom lands of Southern and Central Georgia as I.

Climbing these ridges, part of a convoy of slowly moving trucks and cars, we traveled with almost glacial slowness. (I did not intend a pun, but this rough land is where the glaciers stopped on their southern crawl, depositing on the edge of the pine forest the last of their cargo of hardwood seeds. Here, a scant few centuries later, the glaciers melted like Napoleon's armies fleeing from Moscow and, a pitiful remnant of their greatness, crawled back North again.)

The snow blew in along the margins of the forest, clogged the roads. Although our car was properly equipped for winter travel—I'd brought chains with me from California and installed them at the first appearance of ice on the streets—most of the cars around us weren't. The next several hours were spent in slow motion; sometimes we would come to a complete stop; once our entire group was forced to backtrack three or four miles. I write "group," for we'd became part of a small convoy which included a double-length Winn-Dixie truck, a pickup with an Irish setter covered by a blanket shivering in the seat next to the driver, a gleaming black Cadillac, its multitude of passengers invisible behind steamed-up windows, and Peri and I in my tiny front-wheel drive Nissan. We started and stopped together, halted at the same rest stops. I was almost regretful when the pickup turned off to go its separate way, the setter looking somewhat more cheerful than it had at the beginning of our journey.

We halted often. Wherever we stopped, the people in the service station, or the store, or the restaurant would look up and say "Peri, is that you? Give us a hug." and hug her for a moment silently without speaking or else go back in the kitchen and say, "Kathy, look who's here," and Kathy would come out and give Peri a friendly squeeze.

Not a lot of time was wasted in introducing me. It would be, "this is my friend, Peter," or "this is Peter, he teaches at the University." (Nothing would be accomplished by my telling Peri, yet one more time, that I was not a teacher, but an administrator. She had not grasped the difference between a professor and a department head, much less the more subtle distinction, in my case, between an Assistant and an Associate Dean.)

"Everyone seems to know you," I'd say to Peri in the car afterwards, hoping to pry loose some part of her life story.

"I've always lived in Georgia," was her invariable lackadaisical reply, so that I didn't have much more knowledge at the finish of our ride than when I'd started.

The end justified the means, at least until we started home again. With plenty of snow about us on the ground, Peri proved adept as I at making snowballs. Our toboggan made trip after trip down the slope, while we experimented with she in front, she behind, she on top and she on bottom to find the ideal combination of speed and safety. "It's better if I land on you," she said and I thought so too.

We spent the night in a friend's cabin; a boy, only a few years older than my oldest daughter, his wife, and their child were our hosts. I don't recall Peri calling ahead, but the couple did not seem surprised to see us. As usual, only cursory introductions were made.

Peri and I had a room of our own, though until bedtime we stayed out in the living room with the others. Here, Peri played endlessly with the child; the husband and wife kept disappearing into the bedroom giggling, and I stared into the large wood fire that had been crackling in the fireplace even before our arrival.

Only once was our idyll interrupted. At dinner, Peri had somehow and contrary to her custom led the conversation around to my job and my problems with the chemistry laboratory. I laid it out for them, though they hardly seemed the type of people that would be interested, and they came back with an answer that surprised me.

"Put it in writing," the man said. "Document all the problems. Send a copy to your superior and keep a copy for yourself."

"You've got to protect yourself, Peter." the wife said, backing up her husband.

I looked around the tiny cabin and out the window to the snow-laden trees. Cover your ass. Sage advice from a backwoodsman. And I hadn't. Sent the cover-your-ass this-is-what-is-wrong-with-the-chem-lab memo yet, though it had been typed and laying on my desk for some time.

The next day, as we once again trailed a convoy on the long slow ride back down from the mountains, I asked Peri who those people were. "My son," she said, "his wife and my grandchild. Isn't she adorable?"

I took it she meant the grandchild. "She is," I said, "as adorable as the grandma."

Peri a grandmother? Scratch her to find a grandbaby cooing behind the nursery door? Peri must be at least five or six years younger than I and I'd never considered the possibility of being a grandfather. Who was this quiet little woman asleep in the seat by my side? What other mysteries would slowly unfold about her?

Chapter 17.

I plunged again into the green depths, only to encounter a hard porcelain surface when I hit the shallow bottom; a series of distorted silent black faces looked down at me from the opaque air above, while I twisted, struggled, tried to break away. I woke screaming.

And began to talk, apropos of nothing, about the efforts I'd made learning to surf, the weekends and afternoons I'd spent just learning to turn the board around. Sitting up in bed, for I could not get all the air I needed lying on my back, I told Peri how I used to practice with my board on the floor of the living room, leaping suddenly to my feet, then down on the carpet again. Up, down, up, down. Drove my ex crazy, me repeating the gesture over and over again. Then, one day, I was in the ocean practicing. As always, the practice consisted mainly of my fighting my way out through the surf to where I could misjudge the incoming crests. This time was the long-wished for exception. As I turned around exhausted to face the shore my board was caught by the peaking wave. I stood up quickly just as I'd rehearsed so many times and slid gloriously down the curl. The ride lasted forever, a few seconds outside of time. A short distance off the shore, I pushed off from the board, and fell back in the cold water like a child.

Peri said nothing; half sitting, half lying, her head against my chest, her warm breath heating and arousing my nipples. Was she riding the wave, too, in her imagination, side by side with me on the board?

I did not go out again immediately after my first successful ride, but staggered back to the shore, my body drained of all energy. For perhaps fifteen minutes, I sat upright on the sand, still in my wet suit, looking back out to where the other surfers continued to ride and soar. By the time my power returned, the waves that had given me my first glorious ride had subsided. I went home. But the next day and the next, I rode the curl looking for and always finding the joy I'd experienced in my first wild ride.

Peri and I made love then, and fell asleep holding each other.

An hour or so later, I heard her moving about in the kitchen. She brought me a glass of orange juice—breakfast, she said, would be ready soon—and the paper—that of the previous evening and I just let it lie. I had memories to sort through—the ones I wanted to keep, the surf, our lovemaking, and the dream of disaster in a porcelain pool that I wanted to forget.

I ate a hearty breakfast, devoured everything Peri put in front of me, then made myself more toast, raided the refrigerator, cut a wedge of cheese and attacked the previous night's leftovers.

"It's a wonderful feeling, surfing," I said, ignoring the other unwanted topic, "It's like sex, the waves as responsive as your partner."

Peri touched my large hand with her small one. She was not often given to gestures, so the few she made held special meaning for me. "You had a bad dream," she said, "that's all," and her eyes looked up inquiring into mine.

"I dreamed about the boy. Steven Marshall. The one who died in the swimming pool at the beginning of the term."

"You told me his father was coming to campus?"

"Today. They asked me to talk with him. I'm not sure why. Steve was planning to be a doctor, his father says, so I would have got to know the boy eventually."

"But you didn't know him."

"No, I never had a chance."

Peri gradually led me into the living room and sat me down on the couch. Automatically, I put my legs up on the coffee table. She put her head against my shoulder. "Tell me more about surfing," she said.

"I, uh... I don't want to talk about it right now."

"Then make love to me."

"But we... that is we just."

She leaned upon my chest and kissed me and guided my hand to her breast. I came erect instantly and carried her into the bedroom. So much for age and its lengthening refractory period.

I never talked to Peri about my own near drowning. The circular rip tide that engulfed me once when I was body surfing in Ocean Beach near San Diego.

I was not really conscious of the rip tide's presence. One moment I was close to shore—with just a few more strokes, I could put down my legs and walk, hop the rest of the way to the beach—the next, I had drifted sideways with a further ten yards or more to go before I landed.

It was like ... What I'm trying to describe is... The classic riptide is a brown river, straight as an arrow outward, leveling a path through the waves from the shore to the far horizon. This riptide was different, a whirlpool that carried me around and around in an arc only a dozen yards wide. I was helpless, yet only ten feet away hundreds of swimmers were frolicking in the surf.

"It was your eyes," the lifeguard told me, "I was watching you through the binoculars, and all of sudden your eyes seemed to lose contact with everything around you."

The lifeguard had come walking out to me through the surf; a stout rope around his waist anchored him to the tower and kept him from being swept away.

I'd seen him walking out, had thought, oh, he's come to rescue someone, but had not once suspected he'd come to rescue me. I took the end of the line he tossed me, and though I still had power in my arms and legs, I more or less let him drag me into shore.

My wife and daughters watched all this from the hotel window. "We knew you were in trouble," Samantha told me later. They'd seen me circling around and around and noticed my lack of progress. My wife said the lifeguard had started out for me at the same instant my family decided to go down and get help.

They'd gotten dressed—or at least my wife had, the kids were all ready to go, had been for hours—and reached the beach just as the lifeguard and I touched the shore.

So my little family hugged me—and I hugged them back—while the lifeguard filled out his report.

Their images dance in front of me now—my funny, short little daughters. Like all small children, their heads were large and out of proportion to their bodies. Marilyn, my middle daughter, had just got her first pair of eyeglasses. Age four, her nose was too small to support the frames and her glasses generally hung far down at the tip until she pushed them back up with a finger. Today, full grown, my daughters—the shortest is 5'7," make men's heads turn.

These circuitous thoughts occupied the road from Pineville to Fort Lee and then, abruptly, I was past the line of tenements, in the college parking lot, and swinging my Nissan into its slot.

Donald Marshall, "call me Darren," he asked, was a light-skinned mulatto; slender, about 5'9," a lot smaller than his fire-breathing reputation suggested. I told him essentially the same thing I'd told Peri, that I'd never had a chance to meet his son before the unfortunate accident. He said this was all right, he was just talking to different people on campus, trying to get a picture of what actually happened that night. He told me I had a good reputation and he thought that Steve, his son, would have profited from training in my department. "I think you would have liked Steve too," he said. I assured him that I would have and offered to give him a tour of the facilities. He declined, saying this really wasn't why he had come; he was more interested in what I had seen and what I knew about his son's death.

Embarrassed, I admitted I hadn't known about the death until I read the newspaper the next evening.

"That's what a lot of people here have told me," he said. "It's almost as if the University authorities spent a whole twenty-four hours trying to hush things up and then found they couldn't."

"I.. I... I'm sure that wasn't the case."

"Really, Professor? My son couldn't swim. He was afraid of water, though I'd offered to teach him to swim many times. Then tell me, what the hell he was doing in a swimming pool at twelve o'clock at night."

I don't know what the hell his kid was doing in the pool, I told Peri that evening. I didn't know what to say or how to condole him about the son whom I'd never met. I knew a lot was going on that I didn't know about, a lot that the people I worked with at the college had been keeping from me.

Peri put her hand on my arm, almost as if she were gentling a horse. "Find out, but only if you've got time," she said, "you already do so much."

I never had enough time at school to do all that needed to be done, would never have enough. My staff worked double shifts because our classrooms and laboratories were too small. We lacked support staff, had only unreliable student workers and a secretary who was never present (and was useless if she was). But Steve's father, Darren, had made time for his son. I could, too, if only to pick up the pieces afterward, to find out why and how Steven had died.

Chapter 18.

I started to talk to my colleagues about Steven Marshall's death, going out of my way to visit others and to get them talking. My dream of death and drowning had triggered these inquiries as much as Darren Marshall's visit. Perhaps other people were bothered by his son's death, perhaps they also wanted to talk about it, wanted to know why and how it had happened.

Could Steven Marshall's death really have resulted from a fraternity hazing, I asked my friend Achmed the next day.

My friend Achmed does not answer questions directly; his is a style very different from my own. He prefers not to offend, and to discuss solutions rather than problems—not a bad approach to life. Sometimes, I find his circumlocutions exhausting, but he is very bright, and simply by watching how he goes about solving his problems, I have learned a great deal about solving my own.

"Hazing is a terrible problem on this campus. For a week or more, good students turn into bad students. 'Why do you care?' I ask them, 'Why is joining this fraternity so important to you?' Hazing affects the seniors as well as the freshmen. The members of both groups are withdrawn, apathetic by the end of the week, with big circles under their eyes. They sit quietly in the classroom, but they are not really there."

"But do they hurt one another?" I asked.

"They hurt themselves. They ignore their studies for a week and spend the rest of the quarter catching up. You know, every so often, I think I have a good student, a great one. He'll get a good job, I think, or she'll get a good job, though the girls here have their own separate sets of problems. Then, with only a few months to go, they get caught up with this hazing. They don't show up for a job interview or their grades dip suddenly."

"I would think that President Benjamin...," I began but Achmed interrupted, "he dresses well."

"But being an educational leader," I persisted.

"His educational theories never get put into practice." Achmed finished for me.

I would not be stopped. I said, "Not true. What about the basic training before the semester starts?" Here I referred to the pivot of the Benjamin educational system, two weeks of intensive twelve-hour days each fall before the start of the regular semester during which our incoming students are drilled in study habits and the 3 R's as if they'd never been to school before.

"The students show up, but the professors are never ready. The prep has no curriculum, perhaps half a day's worth of study materials at best. Mostly, the students sit in large classrooms and talk just as they did in high school."

"But the system has been in place for ten years."

"Yes," said Achmed, "For ten years." His message was clear. He had been at the campus for ten years, I for less than one. When I fully understood the situation, I too would tend my own garden.

Then Achmed did a puzzling thing. He touched me; just his hand on my arm, and not that I really minded, I'm pretty much of a touchie-feelie person myself, particularly with my own family; it was just that it was so unusual for him to do so. Achmed stands close to you when he talks, much closer than the average American, but he doesn't touch.

Still with his hand on my arm, he put his face only a few inches from mine and gazed at me intently. "You feel for this person, this student don't you?"

I laughed nervously. "What do you mean?" I asked.

"Perhaps, I should not say any more."

"Please, please."

Achmed stroked his jaw thoughtfully as if still trying to make up his mind. "This concern is unusual, is good. You are a good man. But you do not have much feel for the feeling."

So much for East meets West; they do not understand us at all.

Jewel Larrson, Peri's aerobics instructor, call me "Jewels," had another perspective on Steven's death. Among her many and varied sources of income, Jewel was the girls basketball coach at BC. "The only basketball team, I've ever coached," she confided, "where we have a separate bench for the player's children."

Black men, she said, abused black women and black men abused each other. Serious injuries were not uncommon during hazing week, with students showing up at the hospital emergency rooms with brushed and battered bottoms and, not infrequently, broken fingers and toes. Remarkably, these bruises were sources of pride, just as a woman who had been handed from fraternity brother to fraternity brother so that, in the end, she could not name the father of her child, would take pride in what had been done to her.

Sorority hazing followed a different pattern, the girls would be made to dress funny or leave cold cream on their faces when they appeared in public. "They leave the real abuse to the men," Jules said.

Could the student who was killed in the natorium have been killed in a hazing ritual? "Why else would they have been in the pool that late at night? They probably held his head under too long, the damn fools, and when they let him up again he just wasn't breathing. He drowned, his friends say. How can you drown with your fraternity brothers all around you?"

I tried several times to discuss her theories with Achmed, but he would not even make a pretense at listening.

"How goes it with your anatomy students?" he would say or "When are you and your beautiful wife going to visit us again?" Achmed always insisted on referring to Peri as my wife. I don't know whether he was giving me advice ("marry her, you fool") or if this was simply another example of his refusal to confront something he found disagreeable.

Merrill Jefferson, my old Berkeley buddy, was willing to talk about the BC system's inefficiencies and his plans for change, but he had little to say about fraternities and hazing, and clammed up completely on the subject of Steven Marshall's death.

"I was in a fraternity at Cal," he told me, "Did you think all us fraternity boys were politically unconscious? I enjoyed it. Did me good. Made a lot of friends."

"But aren't the fraternities different here?"

Merrill gave me a disdainful look.

"The hazing." I persisted.

"I got hazed at Berkeley, so what?"

"Did you get beaten, your backside lacerated with a paddle, your ribs kicked in?"

"What are you talking about?" He looked irritated now and, for the first time since we'd met, almost angry.

"It's happened. Here at Benjamin."

"Never. Don't you believe what you read in the papers." And he walked off slowly, his anger, if he was angry, thoroughly held in check, a respectable, Berkeley-educated Negro in a three-piece suit and tie, the winter overcoat over his arm, his sole concession to the changing climate.

I hollered after him, "But what about the Marshall boy?" but he was gone. The only one remaining in the cold gray quad to hear me was a tall, elderly Negro, a near albino whom I did and did not recognize. A custodian, I hoped, though on this campus even the custodians often held the ear of the highest administrator.

Someday, I will learn to hold my tongue, or to speak softly like Achmed with many circumlocutions. On the way home, I remembered who the elderly Negro was. Mr. Nathaniel, the often-absent controller, the tall stately gray eminence behind the Benjamin throne

Perhaps, I was too unimportant for him to pay attention to. Perhaps. They say God takes notice of even the tiniest sparrow. Why should not the devil be the same way?

Chapter 19.

I hear the click, drag, click, drag of someone limping down the hall. Mz. Washington. Has to be. I check my watch: after five; not bad for Mz. Washington who normally left at 4:30, half an hour earlier than the rest of us.

Mz. W looks, if anything, wearier than ever, her less-than-spotless white blouse stained under the armpits where one can see the black hairs dangling. You're working late," I said.

"I'm tired," she replied and when, after a moment, I still had not made an answering comment added, "I think I'm sick."

"What's the matter?" I asked, strictly as a matter of politeness.

"Heart," she said and pointed to that part of her anatomy that, though hidden beneath her tubular breast, was still on the opposite side of her chest from the heart. "Pain in my chest and in my arm." She pointed to her left arm when she said this and now I was concerned.

"You'd better sit down," I said.

We had been standing together in the long hallway outside my office, bare of furniture except for the occasional door propped open by a wastebasket the janitor had left behind. "Maybe you'd better come into my office, I mean the office they're letting me use."

I led Mz. W into my office, though I did not particularly want her there, and had her sit down in my tilt-back chair exchanging it for the uncomfortable straight chair that I assign to student visitors.

"Just rest for a moment," I said, "Then we'll decide what to do." I got out the campus telephone book and began to look up security. The sweat was beaded on her forehead and just above her full thick red lips. The face would be stunning, I thought abstractly, if she'd just get a proper haircut and put a little expression on her face.

When I looked up again, she was still standing. "Sit," I said.

"Do you know how to give a breast exam?" she asked unexpectedly. Startled, I lost my place in the phone book. I looked up at her over my reading glasses.

"I thinks I got cancer, too," she said. "My sister, she got cancer, in the breast." She held one breast out for my inspection. With the cloth of her blouse pulled back tightly against it, her large nipple was obvious. So help me, I was getting an erection. What should have been tragic was turning into comedy.

"You definitely should get a breast examination, then," I said.

"Dat's why I asked you. You being a doctor."

"I'm, I'm not that kind of a doctor," I stammered, perhaps too loudly and too vehemently.

"But you teach the anatomy," she said, "I'm sacred of that other kind of doctor. I wants you to examine me."

I cast about for some way to change the subject, but it was too late, she had opened her blouse, only needing to slip a single last button through the hole to accomplish this task. A huge dark brown teat emerged from the whiteness.

"Look, maybe I should get you a glass of water."

Her long blood-engorged nipple dangled before my mouth.

"You scared of me or something?"

"Not at all." I stood up. Another instant, and my lips would have bit down on that nipple, I was sure of it. She stood up, too, which left very little room for me between my desk and her now erect figure. Her weariness and her feigned heart attack now seemed part of a distant past.

She looked down past my waist. "That jigger of yours is sure lively."

I'm sure it was. Time to leave, definitely. The least attractive woman I had ever seen was putting the moves on me. She went one move further and put the jigger in her hand. The other hand went around my backside and cupped my ass. Her breasts were pressed against me so I could feel her erect nipples and she began to rub them against me in a circular motion.

"You know what I want you to do," she breathed. "First, you suck my titty and then you sucks my cunt." Not on your life, I thought.

The titty was delicious. The long brown nipple bounced off the roof of my mouth and left no room to breathe in the ocean of warm brown flesh that followed it. My jigger, her word, not mine, was in her hand now and out of my pants where it hadn't been doing either of us any good.

Somehow, we had gotten turned around so that her back was to the desk and mine was to the door. Now she pushed herself up on the desk and lifted her skirts. No panties, just dark hair and gaping pink lips.

"I want you inside," she said, "But first you goin' to lick it, Mr. White Man."

Dr. White Man, I corrected, inanely. But I was licking it without further protest, a moist warmness, saturated in sweat that had been accumulating for days, as great a contrast to Peri's sweet delicate cunt as one could possibly imagine.

When Mz. W had come, to her satisfaction, not mine, she pushed me back onto the straight chair and impaled herself on my shaft, jigger, penis whatever. Titty in my mouth, I was good for only a few short strokes before I came solidly inside her. She came a second time, voluminous, distributing a river of moisture down and across my thighs. "You bigger than most colored mens," she whispered in my ear.

A noise outside the door and I shriveled instantly, not that I wasn't half way to detumescence already. She flipped her skirts down, buttoned her blouse, and was around me and out the door before I could begin to dress myself. "Mz. Ferret," I could hear her saying out in the hallway, "thanks you for comin' t' pick me up."

"No trouble, sister," came that warm, longed-for brown voice in reply. I heard giggles—were they discussing me?—and then the quick click of heels. When, clothing rearranged, I looked out in the hallway a few moments later, the only one in sight was the elderly janitor. He gave me an irritated look, "I's almost finished, I got things to do," he said and shot off down the stairs before I could talk to him.

No use checking up. The classrooms, I was sure, were still chalkless, the waste-chemical baskets in the laboratories still unemptied.

Chapter 20.

Mz. W's reliability did not increase in the days following, except in one significant respect. No longer did she start her departure twenty or thirty minutes before the end of the day. Instead, I could count on her remaining until five with a paperback romance when she would appear punctually in my office demanding and receiving certain privileges.

To avoid her, I tried to arrange meetings with my staff for the late afternoons. Yet, inexplicably, when the hour hand began to point toward five, I would rush to bring these meetings to a close and return to my office.

Peri did not notice anything amiss, though I was arriving home perhaps twenty or thirty minutes later each day than I had before and on a more regular basis. "I miss those nooners of ours," Peri said once, referring to the Tuesdays and Thursdays on which, not having any classes to teach, I would contrive to come home early or perhaps to work entirely at home.

Peri might have noticed something eventually, had not Mz. Washington solved the problem for me; she stopped coming in to work. A mild fuss resulted on day one—apparently she had omitted to tell the student workers, but by day two, things were back under control—to the extent they ever had been—as she would issue orders for the students by telephone from her home. She also began to issue orders to me.

"I lef' that book," she said to me, telephoning in early on the afternoon of the second day. "you 'member that book Ms. Feret loaned to me?"

I transferred the call to her office and ferreted about (no pun intended) until the book was found. "Shall I have one of the students bring it?"

"No you bring it; bring it to me now. I's bored."

I brought her the book. Of course, she took no interest in it and led me immediately into her tiny bedroom smelling of unwashed female where I performed my duties.

This became our pattern from then on. She might appear at the office one or two days a week, briefly, to complain about her health or chin at length with her cronies, but mostly, she stayed at home issuing summonses at irregular intervals to me.

I always complied, giving bizarre excuses for my lateness to Peri, and hating myself, for no equality whatever existed in my relationship with Mz. W. What we did and how long we spent doing it were determined entirely by her.

"Call me Ernestine," she said to me unexpectedly one day.

"And what are you going to call me?" I asked.

"Same as all the colored folk does, that funny white man who walks like a duck."

God.

The ritual was the same each time. I would knock on the door of her tiny cottage set back deep in the woods only to get no reply. I would try the door, open it, then step inside calling softly, 'Ernestine.' Then, making my way through the junk on the floor to the door of the bedroom, I would call her name a second time.

"I's here." The scent of her unwashed female body hung heavily on the air. By scent alone—the shades were drawn, thick heavy curtains screened out the light, I would make my way stumbling to her bed.

There she would be, as if at death's door, propped up on pillows, her long golden hair, matted and tangled, surrounding her face like a halo. One huge brown breast jutted forth from the nightclothes. "Ernestine?" I'd say, bending over her.

"Sit down, sit down on the floor." she'd whisper.

I'd sit down awkwardly, my knees doubled up beneath me; she'd pull my head down to her breast. I'd try to speak, and fail as my teeth teased her nipple and the great swell of breast cut off my supply of air.

"Ernestine," I'd say again when I had broken free.

"Now, stand up."

I'd stand, helpless; no longer in charge over even my body, willing, wanting to do whatever she told me.

She would unbuckle my belt as if I were a child, flipping open the top button of my pants with her long brown fingers and begin to undo the zipper.

Then came indescribable pleasure as she took my penis in her mouth. But she was only teasing, her long tongue gliding once, twice, up and down my member before she released me once again. "Now youse slip in beside me in the bed."

I'd slip in beside her, burying my face between her breasts, sucking steadily on each nipple, until she pushed my head down between her thighs. I'd lap for what seemed like hours at her great cunt, almost drowning in the flood of her juices. Only at the very end would she allow me to climb on top of her, my mouth on her mouth, and penetrate her. Grasping a giant breast with each hand, I'd utter a huge, grateful sigh of relief each time I slid back and forth inside her, while she cooed beneath me as if I were her child. My strokes would grow shorter and shorter until, inevitably, hopelessly, thankfully, I came, one last satisfying thrust, my own juices still less copious than her own.

"You can come back tomorrow," she would say and let me slip away.

One afternoon, I arrived at her small cottage in the woods, only to find her minding a seven-year old boy.

"My nephew LeRoy," she said. I was both afraid and relieved that Leroy would put an end to the plans for that afternoon, but no LeRoy wouldn't mind if we went into her bedroom for a while. "Would you honey? Jus' sit n' watch television for awhile." Conversely, LeRoy would object if she were away too long, so that while I was allowed, ordered to eat her out thoroughly; I was not permitted to obtain my own satisfaction. "I bes' get back to the chile," she said, "Tomorra, you come tomorra."

I drove home in a fever, racing over the backcountry roads, picked Peri up at her office and rushed her into bed.

Another day, a knock on the front door sounded while I was in bed with Mz. Washington, Ernestine, and someone came into the living room. I panicked, but Ernestine said calmly, "I jus' see who it is," and drew on a dirty bathrobe over her tawny frame. I heard laughter from the living room, and for forty minutes was forced to wait in that bedroom for the guest to leave.

"Find a lot to talk about," I remarked acidly when Ernestine returned.

"Mz. Ferret," she said by way of explanation, "She like a sister to me."

And what did you talk about, I wondered, but did not ask that question aloud.

To give Ernestine credit, she did not impose on the rest of my life. I was never called at home, always at the office—she had an uncanny way of knowing exactly where I was on campus, and I was only called on during working hours, never on the weekends. In a sense, Ernestine had simply written her own job description.

I wondered if she'd had similar arrangements with Mrs. Black and Mr. White. I wondered, but never did know.

By the way, don't think that because I slept with my black secretary or was allowed to call her by her first name, that I had bridged the gap between the races. We spoke very little of our other lives. I knew as little of her as I did of Merrill's inner self. I never learned why she' d left Chicago or why she chose to work (or, rather, to not work) as an underpaid secretary at a backwoods university rather than in the profession she'd been trained for. I never learned the exact nature of her relationship with Mz. Ferret or the unknown others at the College who protected her and kept her from being fired.

"You got to be born here to understand us," Tad T, one of the music professors, said to me once, "you got to be part of the community." What he said held not just for the blacks, but for the white community as well. I was and would remain as much an outsider in Pineville as in Fort Lee.

When Ernestine called, I was willing; when she didn't call, I was pleased. More and more she didn't call. She didn't come to work either. But I had my own job to worry about by then.

Chapter 21.

Nathaniel Beecher, Chief Financial Officer of B C, (Mr. "Nathaniel" to most of us on campus, though "Nate" I am sure to his college fraternity brothers, the few that were still alive) was a tall, balding mulatto whose color had been eroded in patches by advancing age, giving him an appearance somewhere between an albino and a West African. He had served B C in one capacity or other through six administrations and three name changes and was the oldest still alert member of the college community.

Nathaniel was the prime target of my new determination to make friends and influence people. My Dean had taken recently to frequent reassurances of his respect and even affection for me. I wasn't misled by his protestations. The underlying message was that however deep that affection, he wasn't going to jeopardize his near-at-hand retirement and almost-guaranteed pension.

"You've done a lot for the College," he conceded, "But you've made a lot of enemies in the process because of the way you've gone about it, heedless to my warnings.

"Add in those recent escapades of yours ..."

(I was uncertain whether my Dean referred to my as-yet-undisclosed affairs with Mz. W and Miss S, my failing 50% of the students in my anatomy class, Professor B's alleged pinching of female students, a recent change in textbooks—I had discarded a self-published collection of obsolescent notes put together by Mrs. Black and sold by her for profit at the College bookstore in favor of a more traditional offering—or my faculty's and my own uniform refusal to volunteer monies for a College fundraiser.)

"Your questioning University policy ..."

(This comment stumped me completely. As always the answer could have been "any of the above." Never in a million years would I have dreamed my Dean was referring to my inquiries into Steven Marshall's death.)

"The memo you sent us about the chemistry laboratory. You know you are simply holding a smoking gun to our head."

Now, that is unfair, I thought, bitterly, and mistakenly opened my mouth to protest, "I was just trying to protect the University from a lawsuit."

The Dean looked exceedingly stern, skin drawn and tight around his lips and forehead, "I'm not the one you should apologize to. What you did left a bad taste in everyone's mouth." (Who, I wondered?) "I won't name names." the Dean continued; he shook his head slowly, then held up his gnarled arthritic hand, "In any event, now is the time for making friends, mending fences. Do a little politicking. The results will be good for us." He smiled.

He talked on some more about seeing the other fellow's point of view and not having an opinion on every subject, but I got the message.

(If just once, he'd stuck up for me. Rather, not for me, but for the changes we'd mutually agreed on. Time after time, he'd left it to me to carry the battle to higher levels, his approval merely a license to batter my head against a bureaucratic wall.

But a necessary one, I found when I tried to go around him once. Not only was I told "no" in the most unsubtle fashion by Beau-Beau Lee, but my Dean excoriated me for half an hour in his office afterward and then refused to talk to me for a week in public. My boss, and yet, amazingly, I liked and wanted to please him.)

Mr. Nathaniel was the obvious starting point for my new policy of niceness and joy. Time after time, the roadblocks I encountered could be traced back to him.

Placing an order at the bookstore for a new text for our beginning biology class—a text chosen to replace Mrs. Black's purloined compendium, I encountered unexpected opposition. The order was lost, found not be in the proper form, "the text was not available," "we don't do business with that publisher," and so forth. When I directed my students to the bookstore at a neighboring private college where the text was to be found in plenty, I was excoriated both by my Dean and by President Benjamin. "We rely on the sale of books as a source of income," said the President. "Why can't you be a team player," said my Dean.

A safety shower for the chemistry laboratory I had ordered after obtaining the three requisite signatures for its purchase (including a special appearance before the University Budget Committee to justify my request) was never delivered.

"This is a must purchase," President Benjamin had said at the Budget meeting, but a month passed and we were no better off. I contacted the distributor: "Why the delay?"

"You never placed the order."

Backtracking the order through purchasing led me to Nathaniel again.

I needed to placate him, but how? What did he stand for?

At an accidental meeting with him outside the administration building—we'd never really been formally introduced—I found myself babbling about a recent success of mine. "By combining efforts with Agriculture, we'll cut costs and add students."

He smiled—was it the reduced expenses or the added income that pleased him—but he said and did nothing by way of further praise or reassurance.

I wondered if it was not me but the color of my skin that offended. Perhaps, he really didn't like white people and only tolerated my presence on campus because someone—President Benjamin, the board of trustees, or the state board of education insisted on my being there. I plummeted in an instant from my lofty post of 'patronizing white liberal' to that of a frightened member of a tiny white minority.

We condition ourselves. On our own, we seek out father figures to placate and please. (Please? No, we placate those we fear, while, hopefully, we still try to please only those we love or respect.) The hostage loves his captor, the maus the cat, the worker big brother. If I only knew what Nathaniel wanted.

In one of Steven King's books, he writes about two cemeteries, one hidden behind the other. The hidden plots are ruled by older, now-almost forgotten Gods. I think these are the same deities that Nathaniel prayed to. A modern man, I knew nothing of the sacrifices these primitive deities require, I only knew that I was afraid. I smiled at him and them. I cut costs. Finger to my cap, I made sure he was regularly supplied with figures and charts. But Nathaniel's smile remained cryptic and I remained far outside his confidence.

That Spring when the rains stopped, finally, the red clay was everywhere. Carved from the road banks by the snows and heavy rains, it was carried from road to town by the March winds. Red clay covered the windowsills. At night, when we left the windows open, it crept about the room, coating every exposed surface the color of dried blood.

In the morning, I saw it streaked across the highway, and by evening when I returned from campus, with the dew long since driven away by the sun, the clay filled the air, sometimes forcing all traffic to a halt and occasionally causing accidents as one car swerved to avoid another and five or six half-blind drivers narrowly missed one another, bumpty-bump, in brief excursions that carried them on and off the road's shoulder.

Chapter 22.

Student workers appear at random intervals bearing phone messages, some timely, some left over from the day before:

The Dean wants to see me at four; the Dean has to cancel, will reschedule at a later date. Merrill Jefferson wants to know if this Friday would be convenient. (He keeps inviting Peri and me to his house for dinner, but Peri, of course, won't come. I want to go—I like this man, and need all the allies I can gather, but he spurns my solo acceptance, insists on Peri accompanying me. What new excuse shall I give?) Achmed cancels our luncheon date. This leaves Miss S alone with me for lunch, then.

Mrs. Black shows up, finally, at a department meeting, still puffing from her lengthy walk up the stairs, only to ignore the agenda and demand, out of sequence, "What Dr. Wood was doing about Career Day?"

No longer a tyro administrator, Dr. Wood replies, unhesitatingly, that he is "making a final review of the plan."

Later that day, when Mz. W also took the trouble to ask about Career Day, I telephoned Dean Holley at home to find out what Career Day was. "Oh, you know, you bring speakers on to campus and they discuss careers."

"When is it scheduled for?" I ask.

"Next week sometime. I've got the calendar around here some place. Everything under control?"

"Couldn't be better." I lie and retreat to my office to think.

Mrs. Becky Mursch, our one and only white female student, she of the too-many, too-frequent complaints, appears briefly at the door. I would have been grateful for the interruption, but, surprisingly, when she saw I was inside at my desk, she quickly ran away.

Martin King, the President of the Student Council came by, I forget the pretext—apple-polishing, I'm sure, was his primary motive—and I decide to sound him out on Career Day. "What do you think we should do?'

"Meet employers, like talk to someone from Pineville Hospital and from Mercy in Atlanta."

Good answer. Unlike most of our students, Martin, a prospective physicians' assistant, has a very clear idea of his career goals. "Like the chief administrators at the hospital," I suggest.

Martin looks puzzled, "Usually, they bring in somebody to campus from Personnel."

A surprisingly smug smile crossed my face. "Not this time. We're going straight to the top."

Martin looks at me, his gaze for once filled with unfeigned admiration. "You can do that?" he exclaims, adding quickly, "I didn't mean that the way it sounds."

"Piece a cake," I reply confidently. "We'll even bring them here for lunch. I'm going to need some help though. We've got a lot of work to do and not much time."

"I'll call a meeting," Martin suggested. Martin was always calling meetings, but this time, it seemed to me, a meeting was just the ticket.

Thadeus T, a good bud, a hell of a trombone player, and the director of the University chorus came by then and we went to lunch. Tad T was a funny guy, from the way he walked—both arms swinging forward simultaneously, head bobbing like a toy monkey—to an endless fund of anecdotes told in a variety of dialects. I don't know which was funnier, his Newt Gingrich, his Ronald Reagan, or his Beau-Beau Lee.

Today, the topic was his job. "It's hell," he said, "trying to teach a chorus that can't read music."

"But they sound wonderful," I replied. (I'm a pushover for choral music of all kinds, from a third-grade Super Choir preparing to go on a tour of local nursing homes to Atlanta's Robert Shaw chorale that I've already taken Peri twice to hear. The Benjamin chorus, filled as it was with rich resonant voices, lay somewhere between.)

"Our students have wonderful voices," Tad conceded, "but they've memorized all their music. Give them something they haven't sung in church and they completely fall apart."

"So much for honoring the music of Ed Blaine and Florence Price."

"Who?" Tad T said.

Martin K held his meeting and the kids talked for hours, cutting numerous classes in the process. In the end, the students came up with four different plans:

a) a resume bank (which died stillborn when no student submitted a resume even after an intensive afternoon session—taught by me—on resume preparation),

b) a job bank (another widely endorsed idea that despite a plethora of volunteers was never brought to fruition),

c) a "meet-your-future-boss" lunch which was, with the one exception I'll describe shortly, an unqualified success, and

d) a tour of Atlanta's major medical employers which, but never mind.

The lunch was a simple to organize—thanks to Peri's help—and was simply a question of inviting representatives of Pineville's leading medical employers, all of whom were white, to meet with our students, all but two of whom were black.

I told Peri I didn't want people from human resources and she more than obliged. I got a physician (two of them actually, one the chief administrator at the local hospital, the other the head of the local public health department), a dentist (who talked about careers for hygienists and dental assistants), and a guy who ran a medical-supply distributorship out of his garage but said he was overdue for a big expansion. All were clients of the answering service Peri worked for.

The lectures were given to a packed house but, mysteriously, two-thirds of the students had melted away by the time of our sit-down face-to-face lunch. Martin King was at the table, naturally, in the seat adjacent to the hospital administrator, but Doreen, who had been among the most tireless of those students who helped to put the program together, was not.

Later that afternoon, I asked Doreen why she had not come to the lunch (which was outrageously successful, by the way, and led to a dozen of our students getting interviews and/or job referrals). "I just wanted a hamburger," she said, which made no sense at all to me.

I asked Achmed if he could explain this seeming paradox. "Many of our students come from really poor homes. Their parents aren't college graduates, but sharecroppers who never finished school. The students don't know how to hold a knife and fork, and worse, they know they don't know and are ashamed."

I was ashamed, too, that I hadn't understood and planned for this possibility. But what can you expect from a white man who walks like a duck?

More than I could expect from the students, I discovered three days later when the Great Atlanta Tour got under way.

Chapter 23.

Career Day dawned bright and clear. The buds were out on the trees and the scent of new growth was everywhere. What ever happened to winter?

I brushed my teeth, thanked Peri for fixing breakfast, and kissed her goodbye. "Have fun on your field trip." she said. It's not a field trip, I corrected her inwardly for the third or fourth time; it's a get-to-know-the-white-folks-that-do-the-hiring experience. But her mind was stuck back in junior high; for her, a trip away from school it would remain.

At 7:00, I stood outside the '76 gas station, waiting. Our first appointment in Atlanta was for nine. We could leave a half hour late and still make it. At 7:45, still waiting with nary a student or a bus in sight, I called Peri. "Anybody telephone me from the school?" I asked. "Nope." At 8:00, I headed for home; Peri would be going to work and someone should be by the phone to field emergency calls.

At 8:20, I was back at the '76, fretting, my left eyelid working on a nervous tic. At 8:30, I hit the road, working on my apology, and risking ticket after ticket as I sped to Atlanta.

9:35 a.m. and I strode through the corridors of Mercy Hospital exuding false confidence. The administrator, a tall balding man, his suit jacket and tie just visible through the folds of his lab coat, shook my hand firmly. I looked him straight in the eye and then, casting my eyes floorward, mumbled, "We've had a problem."

"Where are the students?" he inquired jovially.

"We've had a vehicle problem," I improvised. "They asked me to go on ahead and extend our apologies."

"Should we wait for them, then?"

"Oh." The reader should insert a longish pause at this point, perhaps stopping to brainstorm with other readers as to how the protagonist, me in this instance, could best extricate himself from the situation. I said, "Oh," a second time, and added, "We're on such a tight schedule, I'm afraid the bus has been sent on to our next stop."

The administrator shook his head sympathetically. "What a pity. But why don't I show you around. Do you have the time?"

Nothing but, I thought, until the hour arrives for my next groveling apology. A whole day of spurious visits and improvised lies stretched before me. Seven stops had been arranged, five that day and two the next, and all would have to be honored. "Yes, thank you very much."

The tour of the hospital was wonderful. Dr. Anderson, the administrator, was very gracious. "Open-heart surgery," he said, as we looked down at the operating theater from the overhead window, "A very tricky procedure. Not quite as straightforward as we surgeons would like you to believe." I saw x-rays and heard them being interpreted by a group of radiology residents; we visited the morgue; we even went on rounds. "I might not have done this if you'd brought all your students with you." In short, Dr. Anderson put together the finest, most informative tour it was possible to assemble—on short notice. And how had we at Benjamin College responded? We'd buggered it up. I knew I'd be taking gas for this one when I returned to Fort Lee. Best to network with Dr. Anderson then, and look forward to my next job.

"What do you know about Atlanta 2000?" Dr. A asked me as I was leaving.

"I'd... I'd like to learn about it."

"Well, if you have time this evening, I think I can give you some firsthand knowledge."

"I'm staying over," I said, improvising once more, "the students really don't need me to chaperon."

"Good. You can even bring a couple of students along if you like. They'll probably appreciate the free meal. Atlanta 2000 is simply a group of leaders in the medical industry and more than a few pure politicians who are trying to plan for Atlanta's future medical needs. We meet once a month." And he gave me the directions to the dinner meeting.

Great, a major opportunity for soon-to-be Benjamin graduates and future leaders of the black community to chin chin with the white establishment. Only none of them had got on the bus.

Or knew how to find me if they had. Had I given out the schedule? No, nothing was in writing. But surely I'd told some of the students about the stops we'd be making. Surely, two or three would show up at the next stop.

It wasn't the next stop, but the next to last when they or, rather, he caught up with me. Only one student, but boy was I glad to see him. "Kermie!" Crippled by premature arthritis, but for his race—Caucasian, and color—white, an altogether fitting symbol for Benjamin College. Together, we toured a medical-supply wholesaler, then formed a caravan to our last stop, a maker of specialized electronic equipment for use in intensive-care wards.

Their factory was a paradise for anyone up on electronics jargon, impedance, printed circuits, and software on a chip. The engineers didn't seem to care if anyone listened to them or not, so Kermie and I had a chance to exchange notes.

He'd gotten up late, par for a Benjamin student, and arrived late at what he'd assumed was the designated meeting point, a '76 station near his home, and thus convenient for him, although three exits up from the actual gathering spot. When no one else showed up, he'd gone home, consulted his notes and followed me on the tour, arriving late, but less and less so at each successive stop. They'd even given him his own tour at Serogen, a commercial blood laboratory that had equipment Benjamin students and faculty could only dream of.

We get a free dinner tonight, I told him, which seemed to cheer him up. His own wild car ride from Benjamin had not set well with his arthritis and he admitted to being in pain as he swallowed an Advil. But pale and twisted though he might be, he was a Benjamin student and he was there with me in Atlanta, which seemed to prove, to me, that it could be done.

Chapter 24.

Despite its successful conclusion, I did not win any trophies for the career day I'd arranged. My Dean was not on campus the next day nor was he there for the remainder of the week. His absence, perhaps not due to chance alone, enabled me to communicate directly with his superior, the Vice-President of Academic Affairs, Beau-Beau Lee. "How did this happen?" Beau-Beau wanted to know.

I told Beau-Beau I would be happy to write a report.

"Just tell me."

I said I still wasn't quite sure why the students hadn't met me as agreed on. I explained about living in Pineville, adjacent to the Interstate, and about the arrangements I'd made with Martin, the student who would be driving the bus, to meet me there. Beau-Beau put his face and bulk close to mine.

"You should have been on campus to get the tour started." A stubby brown finger was raised to within inches of my nose. "Our students aren't exactly like other students. They need extra encouragement, the sort of extra encouragement that, frankly, we expected your high price tag would provide."

There wasn't much I could say to this, not without turning in my resignation.

When I tracked down Martin, the student who had been supposed to drive the bus, his explanation did little to allay my anxiety, filled as it was with ill omens for my future.

"I got the bus all right, but none of the students wanted to come. I begged with them, pleaded with them, but they all said they had other things to do. Doreen said she'd come if Natalie would, and Natalie said it would depend on Robert and it was getting later and later and finally I just drove over to Pineville to meet you."

"What time was this?

"Quarter past eight."

At a quarter past eight, I'd been back in my home waiting for his call. "So what happened when you got to the 76 station?"

"I looked for you. You wasn't there. So I drove back to the campus."

I interrupted. "Why didn't you just phone me at home? I gave you my number."

"That's what I was going to do, phone you."

I shook my head; "You could have used the phone in the gas station"

"Oh. They lets me use the phone on campus for free. And when I gots back Doreen and Natalie and Robert were all ready to go."

And so Martin King had spent over an hour driving back and forth between Pineville and Fort Lee to save twenty cents. Of the twenty-five students scheduled to appear at the student union at seven, only four had actually put in an appearance, three of them over two hours late.

Beau-Beau Lee did not want to hear this explanation.

Within hours, the situation grew still more complicated. All the female students were withdrawn from my classes, and not just mine, but Professor B's and Mr. White's as well. I had a terrifying sense of deja vu. Why was this happening? What was the reason? And Ms. S had disappeared. Between scrambling to find someone to cover her labs and those of Mr. White, who seemed also to have vanished, I had little time to wonder about the mystery of the missing coeds, but I knew I would soon find out.

Mrs. Black put in an appearance at the department office grinning, but, to give my Ernestine credit, Mrs. Black was given short shrift when she tried to rag on me. "He doin' the best he can," was what I was told Ernestine had said, and I suppose this was the best I could expect in my defense.

That evening, I had so much I wanted to discuss with Peri. My whole life to be honest, from the disaster at Flagstaff College when I was twenty-one to the present day. But I wasn't sure what to leave out. If I did talk about Flagstaff, even omitting the part about the stack of Playboys and the three coeds who had initiated me into sex, then she might think, oh he's up to the same tricks again at Benjamin. And I wasn't—not as far as the students were concerned. I was as innocent with them as I'd been at Flagstaff before the fall. More so, because at Flagstaff, lust had been ever present in my heart. While at Benjamin, I'd never given my students a second glance. Apart from their being black—all right, Ernestine was an exception—they weren't much older than my daughters. Sex with a student was unthinkable for me.

The problem of Ms. S's disappearance remained, nagging at me even as I longed for sleep. Where had she gone? And where was Mr. W?

The answers arrived the next day, though not quite on time.

The weekly meeting of the chief administrators was scheduled for one p.m. I wasn't invited, but then I'd never been invited before; the one p.m. meeting was for top brass only. This time, though, I took my rejection personally. I was meant to. My Dean had gone out of his way that morning to tell me I wasn't to come.

Normally, the weekly meeting began at two. This week, the meeting was scheduled to begin thirty minutes early. Why? Was it because I would be in class at two p.m. and they wanted to fire me before class started?

I needed to relax. This shouldn't have been a problem; I know dozens of relaxation techniques: Read a book. Go to the gym and do chin ups and jumping jacks. Run a half-mile on the track. Get out the saxophone and practice scales and finger exercises.

The problem was that by 1:30 pm, I'd tried every one of those techniques and needed something else, desperately, to divert my attention from my impending doom. I sat down for a moment in the shade on a raised concrete planter where two of my female students Kitisha Morgan and Havanne Jones were sipping Dairy Queen and talking ten to the dozens.

At least, they were talking till I sat down and, then, silence.

"You don't need to worry about my listening in," I called out, and then began to worry myself about why they were worrying. Had the jungle telegraph—no racist slur intended—already reached out and told them the results of the meeting, or was it simply that I was white and they were black. "You're not talking about anatomy, I gather," I said, pompously, just to have my mouth moving.

Havanne snorted.

"We talking bout boys," Kitisha said.

"Well I'm one of them, or was." I did my best to show my teeth in a real smile.

"You a wool," Havanne said.

I looked and was puzzled. "You know, like a father," Kitisha said and pointed to her head.

A wool. I touched my salt-n'pepper head. Not race discrimination, but age. "Thanks girls," I said, and got up out of the shade. Their lips began to move almost as soon as I'd left the shadow of their tree.

I ran into Martin King on the path, accidental on my part, deliberate on his, and practiced being calm and cool, pontificating about job possibilities. "Bring me your resume," I said, "I'll look it over."

1:45. My own, recently granted office, a renovated broom closet, was windowless. At the far end of the hallway above the stairs, a lone opening looked out across the quadrangle toward the administration building. I peered through it. No one was walking this way.

I heard a step behind me in the hallway! Was it Mz. W, bringing the bad news: "They wants to talk to you in the President's office." No one. Just the scamper of tennis shoes as a student disappeared down the stairs on his own errand.

The valiant only die but once, the coward dies a thousand times. Tell me about it.

At 2:00 pm, I entered the anatomy laboratory. "Do we have a quiz, Professor Good?"

"No. No. Not today."

I walked amongst the trial men in a suit of shabby gray and, suddenly, began to realize they weren't going to fire me after all. The afternoon meeting of the administrators was, had to be, about something else. One by one, the missing girls reappeared, slipped on their stained beige lab coats and took their place with the others.

Did you ever notice how when the pressure is lifted, you overshoot, begin to babble, enter a totally unjustified state of euphoria? I knocked a skull off the table before I calmed down.

"You wants us to take care of it, Professor Wood?"

No. No. My fault. And as I swept poor Yorick into the trash bin, I resolved to drive home that day at speeds no greater than 50 mph, to slow down in everything I did until I was myself again.

Not till after five, and, then, only because of an accidental meeting in the parking lot, did I learn what had actually gone on during the past day and a half. I learned from the Dean that it was Becky Mursch, our lone white female student, who had originated the complaint of sexual harassment. Another attempt to get her husband's attention. She had filed formal complaints against me, against Professor B, and against Mr. W. And recanted all three complaints the next day. "Her stories just didn't hold together," the Dean told me (much later), at the same time, leaving me with the impression that Beau-Beau Lee and Mr. Nathaniel—who had somehow gotten into the act—had done their best to try to make her stories fit.

The interrogations of the female students had elicited little or nothing. "He not much of a teacher," one of the students complained about me, "he go too fast." Another said, "I had it in for colored people." But the Dean assured me no one had taken this latter complaint seriously.

They'd interviewed the female instructors, too. Apparently, Ms. S had broken down during her interrogation, bursting into tears and then, when left alone for a minute, had run from the room.

I went to her apartment that evening—I know, I know, this was a dreadful tactical mistake. Her door was locked, but from what I could make out through the curtains, the apartment had been vacated hurriedly. Her closet door was open and it looked as if many of her clothes were gone.

Mr. White showed up in my office early the next morning. His explanation for his disappearance was a simple one. He was guilty as hell. Not with Becky M, of course, he'd have been hard pressed, even for the major cocksman he fancied himself to be, to have pushed in that direction, but it seems he had gotten one of our girls pregnant.

"And?" I pressed him.

"And I thought maybe she turned me in."

She hadn't, I found out later. Mr. White, Ray, Raymond, now my buddy for life, kept me updated. The girl's story of her pregnancy—yes, she'd tried that out on her professor lover, had been a complete fabrication designed to entice him to leave his wife and move in with her. Having been in this situation before, White had simply withdrawn from the scene, Dean Holley style, and waited to see how events developed.

I thought of warning White to stay away from the girl, for his own good and hers—wasn't this my obligation as his department head?—

but realized, in time, how useless such a warning would be, how pompous it would sound. I had too many hassles in my own life without needing or wanting to help others with their problems.

Chapter 25.

After a seemingly indefinite number of postponements, dinner at Chez Jefferson was finally on for Peri and I. She sat at her dressing table in a flesh-colored half-slip painfully installing layers of unnecessary makeup. "You look fine just as you are," I said, and when she ignored me, added, "You never use makeup."

"I think it's appropriate." Her lips became too crimson and her light blue eyes, lighter and paler than a bird's egg, were rendered colorless by aquamarine eyeliner. Why not streak her hair, put a ring in her nose, crayola on her cheeks, which she did, touch up her cheeks with rouge, that is.

The final crippling touch was an overdose of some incredibly toxic perfume. "But you never wear perfume."

"I always use perfume," she replied, which she did, I guess, the light scent of mountain lilacs, the scent that I thought of as hers. Now, this new odor asaulted my nostrils, unpleasant, excessive, and disturbing.

"I don't like it," I said. "Too much," I said.

"Then you won't be trying to drag me down on the bed again, mussing my clothes." And I wouldn't, not until she washed that stench off.

The Jefferson's had moved the previous year to the north of Fort Lee, on a large newly-tracted section of land, where, not surprisingly, the homes of President Benjamin and Beau-Beau Lee were also to be found.

The tract had once been home to a pecan grove; a few of the tall broad-limbed trees could still be seen along its edges, but on the tract, itself, the trees had been leveled and the ground left barren and exposed. I would not have wanted to live there.

I treasured the few trees that grew outside our cottage in Pineville—a willow and several magnolias, and though we had the tiniest of front yards, with nothing at all in back, Peri had somehow contrived to cover the vacant space with flowers, whether in pots upon the front porch or along the earth-filled margins.

The Jefferson's had the lawn—no denying its blue-green majesty—but the few flowers by the front door seemed out of place and in back, only a few withered roses and two staked tomato plants had survived the sun's awful toll.

Peri held my hand as we headed up the walk, then, at the last minute, transferred her hold and her weight to my arm. "You know I've never been in a colored person's home before."

"Blacks," I admonished reflexively, but for once didn't launch forth on some kind of lecture. I'd never been in a black person's home either.

The Jefferson house was straight out of my youth, the ultimate in '50's kitsch. It would have not have surprised me if I'd found a pile of plastic slipcovers in their closets, removed only seconds before our arrival.

We made light conversation, complimenting the Jefferson's on their home, nibbled on too salty peanuts, ignored some kind of white cheese. Mrs. Jefferson, Melanie, seemed to be familiar with everything that was happening at the school, and Peri, despite what I'd assumed was a sincere lack of interest in college affairs, also seemed to know all the gossip. (Who had told her? She certainly hadn't learned the details from me. Any mention of Benjamin College had been enough to drive her from the room.)

At supper, we were introduced to the Merrill's two children, the two that remained at home, a boy and a girl, teenagers.

"John will be going to Athens in the fall," Merrill's wife said proudly. The boy, a tall gangly youth, took mainly after the mother with some slight concession to Merrill's long narrow nose and Kirk Douglas chin.

"He wants to get away from home," Merrill put in quickly as if to explain this defection from Benjamin. All kids seem to want to get away from home these days, I conceded, and then (admitting I looked forward to this day) come back to live with their parents once the world has dealt them a cruel blow or two.

Another son and his wife had been expected for dinner, but couldn't make it; something had come up at the last moment, Melanie rushed to inform us. Merrill glowered, so I supposed he'd wanted the boy to come and the boy simply hadn't complied. Was it that the boy or his wife had objected to us, two white people, in their parents' home?

Dinner didn't bring Merrill and I any closer together. Somehow, I'd imagined that when I visited his house, we would talk more as friends than as colleagues. But the professorial air that Merrill wore like a second vest was with him still, though he made a pretense of looking casual, if not relaxed, in a golfing shirt, slacks, and Weejums. "We're friends aren't we?" my voice kept asking, whatever my actual words.

Dismayed and hurt by his indifference, I turned on Peri. "I'm surprised you know so much about campus." I said in a whining tone.

"Well, of course, she does," Mrs. Jefferson, Melanie, now, to both of us, put in quickly. "How could she help but know, with you bringing home all the news. And of course, there's that friend of hers."

Friend? I looked inquiringly at Peri who was staring, lips pursed, at Mrs. Jefferson. Melanie glanced quickly at her husband. I saw no change in Merrill's expression, but some signal must have been exchanged, for she changed the subject.

"You met Dad at college?" Merrill's daughter asked when her mother brought up the Berkeley connection. "I guess, I don't think of Dad as ever actually having gone to college, I mean as a student, that is."

Merrill laughed. "You think I always had gray hair?

"Tell me, Professor Wood, what do you think of Merrill Jr. going to Berkeley rather than Athens?"

"Not a good idea," I began, and we were off on a furious discussion that took us through to dessert—peach cobbler fresh out of the oven with ice cream.

"Do you play whist?" Merrill asked after dinner. It was not really a question; he led us to a combination family-room study where two decks of cards, a blank pad of paper, and pencils had already been laid out on a table. At the far end of the room, Merrill's children had gathered around a T.V.; I'd like to have joined them.

"Is it like bridge?" I asked. I was prepared to say I was not much of a bridge player.

"You'll enjoy it," Peri said, taking my arm and leading me to the table. "Leave it to Peter," she said apologetically to Merrill's wife, "and we'd be talking shop all day."

But I like talking shop.

"Merrill's the same way. We'll play whist, I told him. I'm not going to hear again about what you would do if you were the Dean."

"I like whist," Peri said, "Let's be partners."

Mrs. Jefferson beamed and suddenly I was abandoned, left to play a game I didn't know and didn't particularly want to play as partner to the easily-annoyed Merrill.

The game, simple enough, lacked one of bridge's few good points, the opportunity to play dummy and get away from the table once in a while. When Merrill offered to freshen our drinks, I was on my feet in an instant, first to go to the bathroom and then to walk out on the lawn.

I'd made my way along the side of the house to that terrible waste of a garden when I noticed a slim shadow next to me. Phoebe, the Jefferson's youngest child was gazing up at the pale corona of the old moon. She half-turned on my arrival, then turned back, pretending to be oblivious to my presence.

"You're not watching T.V.," I said, one of those dumb things adults say to children.

"No point in my being in there with Mr. Big-Deal-I'm-going-to-college-and-you-have-to-stay-home-with-mom-and-dad."

I grunted, tried to smile sympathetically, tried to bridge the gap between the generations. For a moment, we did share a silence; then, she was gone.

Merrill came out of the house, leaving the back door open. I could hear Peri and Mrs. Jefferson still chattering inside, their voices moving back and forth along a path between the dining room and the kitchen. I smiled, tentatively. Now Merrill and I could talk; but he only lit a cigarette and walked off in the darkness in the direction his daughter had taken.

I followed. After awhile, he began to provide a sort of tour of the darkened yard. He would be putting in roses by the fence—a second time, the first attempt had failed. These were peach trees, just planted. Too dark to see any of these things, really, though he crouched down at one point as if trying to show me an unwanted growth on the end of a shrub.

We'd come all the way round and were headed back into the house when I stopped him. "We don't seem to be friends." I said.

It was true. I was in his home at last, my girl at my side as ordered, and yet we were more distant than ever. What was the cause?

I saw a movement at the window, heard Melanie Jefferson's clear musical voice say, "And of course when Dean Holley retires, and he's got to whether he likes it or not in two years, why Merrill will be Dean."

I looked at Merrill, but could not make out his features; the light from within lit my face, left his in darkness. I knew he knew we were both obvious candidates for the soon-to-be-vacant deanship.

He snorted, "That's not the reason," and stamped out his cigarette. All natural enthusiasm was gone from his voice, withdrawn, withheld from me, "nor is it because of your wife and her relations, though that was my son's excuse for not coming here today. I expected more from you Dr. Wood, that's the reason."

I tried to relax, to loosen my shoulders, to let the air flow naturally in and out of my lungs.

"When you come from Berkeley, you have a certain reputation to uphold. Certain things are expected of you, the way you dress, the way you conduct yourself in public, the way you behave at meetings and in the classroom."

I could not, would not relate to what he was saying. I had a sudden vision of a teaching assistant of mine at Berkeley, appearing for class each day in a suit, but wearing sandals.

"I've accomplished a lot," I said, "The health-science faculty is a step, two steps above any other in the college. The Dean says so, the students say so—you saw the survey—Mercer Medical School says so—we're back on their accreditation list or will be soon."

"So you say."

If we were schoolboys, I would have punched him. We weren't; we weren't even in a bar. I gritted my teeth, smiled evilly and openly, thought, another year and I'm going to be your boss, you bastard.

The two women came out of the house laughing, as carefree as Merrill and I were stiff and apart.

"Lots to talk about," Merrill said. His voice showed the strain.

Melanie beamed. "Oh, we're having a good time. Plenty of girl talk. I've even been teasing Peri about her uncle."

Merrill made a face and a dismissive gesture with his hand, his cigarette ash dancing lightly toward the ground. "Georgia's gone a long way beyond that."

Peri took my hand briefly, pressed it. "I agree," she said.

We walked around the side of the house, back the way I had come. Peri and Melanie had their arms about each other, Merrill and I walked stiffly on either side.

At the front door, Melanie said, "Well Peri Mattox, it's been a pleasure meeting you."

"Me too," said Peri, and to my surprise gave Mrs. Jefferson a brief hug and a light peck on the cheek

Melanie glowed, hugged her back.

"Who's your uncle?" I asked Peri in the car.

"Oh, he used to be Governor," she replied, sleepily. "They were very nice people. You know, I've never been in a Negro's home before. They had such nice furniture. I wonder if we'll be able to afford furniture like that?"

This last was a question, not a statement. I had the money, would have more if I were promoted to Dean; was it to be used for her, for us, or for my kids as I had planned? Did I really have enough money for both an old family and a new?

If I kept my job, that is.

Chapter 26.

Easter. I was going on vacation again and this time I was going with Peri.

I'd spent Christmas with my kids and Peri with hers; it had been my choice, then, for the two of us to be apart; Peri had said she'd come with me to California to visit my family if I wanted her to. I hadn't, then; I wasn't sure she'd fit in with my children, my three college-age daughters who were convinced they were already adults. But when I got out West, though I did spend a lot of time with my children, I also spent an hour on the phone each day talking with Peri. "And when you weren't on the phone with her, you were talking about her, Dad." my oldest daughter Samantha complained, "Bring her with you the next time, will you?"

Good advice that I planned to honor, rich or poor, in sickness and in health.

I was pretty much riding the curl at work, at the peak of my academic career. I finally had a faculty I could feel confidence, even pride in. The students liked me or said they did though I still couldn't begin to understand many of their ways. Their secret names, for example: Robert was really Steve. Latisha was Willie. If I called role using the names in my registration list, no one responded.

Mrs. Black had taken the term off—a "sabbatical" she called it—eliminating the last of the challenges to my authority. I could look in on each classroom and laboratory and be guaranteed a favorable reception. "Is everybody working?

We had a new culture: a class where students laughed and talked openly was a bad class; a laboratory where students scurried about silently trying to keep up with the never-ending pressure, a good one.

(Some of the students were even beginning to joke again—the best of signs, while their eyes and hands remained busy and focused.) The shy, near inaudible Miss S. would simply not have fit in. (She had never returned; I'd received a request from Atlanta for a reference, signed it and sent it on.)

Dean Holley described me as a "problem solver," and while I waited for him to say "and a problem maker," he never did. Still paranoid in his presence, I would wait a moment or two for the bitter part of the sandwich, before realizing that, perhaps, finally, the old and new would blend.

President Benjamin took me aside the week of our departure for the Bahamas and asked if I'd mind making a series of speeches to the white community when I returned from my "vacation." He paused when he said the word, and, so help me, winked.

Perhaps Pineville wasn't as far from Fort Lee as I thought it was.

The Bahamas are every bit as wonderful as they are supposed to be. Long, clean white beaches once you are away from the hotels, plenty of exotic shells to be found, and a child-wife-mistress to be praised each time she found one.

I went snorkeling; Peri waited on the beach with a huge straw hat and a thick layer of sun block shielding her fair skin. She went horseback riding later that day, a tiny figure, dwarfed by and totally in control of the huge beast.

I stayed on my own legs, thank you, and the instant the group walked off down the trail regretted I hadn't gone with her.

But the next day, we took a tour in a glass-bottom boat, and the day after that we took a tour bus inland, and the day after that we went home.

We had barely opened the door to our cottage—closed up for the week, it needed a good airing—I was scurrying about, opening the windows, thinking, now, today, I'm going to ask Peri to marry me, when I heard her in the bedroom, crying.

"What's wrong," I asked, kneeling by the side of the bed.

"We're so different you and I. From the very first day, I've been asking myself, 'Why me, why'd he choose me?' I still don't know."

I tried to touch her, to put my arms around her, but she turned away.

"Peri?"

Her sobs grew louder.

I walked around the house shutting the windows I'd just opened. I made dinner, thawed some frozen scallops and sautéed them in a pan.

"Peri?"

She was sleeping, was sleeping still when I crept into bed beside her.

We'd spent the last week in the bridal suite at the fanciest hotel in the Bahamas, calling room service most mornings, because the view was so terrific and we were so much in love. We come back home. I'm going to ask her to marry me. And she's asleep, hiding.

She was gone from the house when I woke the next morning, but breakfast was warm and waiting in the oven.

Chapter 27.

Several unsettling things occurred on the day I returned to campus.Someone else was parked in my parking space: who? why? this had never happened befor! Then Merrill shot by me on the pathway as if he hadn't seen me, though, normally, I could count on at least fifteen minutes of conversation even when I needed to and told him I must break away.

The Dean wasn't in his office, never a good sign and always a major indication that trouble was in the making and he wanted to be well separated from it. The note on my desk read, 'feel free to call him at home', which, translated, meant solve those problems on your own.

Raymond White, my buddy for life, passed by me on his way to class with his eyes fixed on the ceiling. He didn't speak, not even a nod of his head and carefully kept his back to me when a student stopped to talk with him. Come to think of it, wasn't that Ray's car that had been parked in my spot? They weren't thinking of making him the chairman again? What an insult! Replacing me, the guy who had literally rebuilt Benjamin's prehealth program from scratch, with a man whose doctorate had been earned by correspondence.

Was I or wasn't I fired?

The clincher occurred when I encountered Mrs. Angel in the parking lot at the end of the day. "I'm so sorry," she said in a voice that communicated her sincerity, and then, unexpectedly, she walked across the parking lot and touched my arm.

She'd never touched me before, nor had we actually stood side by side without a counter or a table between us. Once or twice we'd exchanged shy glances as we walked together to our cars. But this was all.

No one has touched me in the past six months. The colored touch one another all the time. From a simple handclasp, to an arm thrown carelessly around another's waist or shoulders when they stand together in groups. But they never touch me.

"Would you like to go somewhere and talk?" Mrs. Angel said. "I'm so sorry, we never really got to know each other. We weren't really very friendly. None of us were."

We went somewhere to talk, but, of course, it really wasn't me she wanted to talk about, but her.

"Follow my car," she said, and I followed her station wagon in my tiny Datsun, little dog behind big, to the west of town.

The road, a new one, led away from Pineville, in the opposite direction to the Interstate, toward the Alabama border. The highway was new to me; the faded farmhouses and the few scattered outbuildings strange and disorienting. I suppose this was why the trip seemed to take so much longer than it actually did. Where are we going, I wondered, as we passed through town after tiny town. Long enough for me to dwell on the thought that this day might well be one of my last ones on campus, that shortly I would receive the formal notice, would be out looking for a job again.

We stopped finally in the parking lot of a small restaurant, "Georgia Bar-B-Q," "Bar," and "Alberts" read the neon signs. Across the road, the Melville Motel, parking lot deserted, waited forlornly for drinkers turned lovers to find their evening of fun.

I got out of my Datsun and walked around to the driver's side of her station wagon. The window slid down and her beautiful face emerged. "Sit down here for awhile and talk," sang her warm contralto voice. She gestured toward the passenger side and, then, seeing that I would have to walk around her car a second time to get there, slid across the seat and made room for me.

I sat down behind the wheel still wondering why we were here. What did she, what did I want to talk about?

"I thought about inviting you to our home, I really did. But Al kept saying, what did we want a white man in our home for. And then when we found out about your girl... is she your girl or your wife? I think everyone wants to know. Al said, 'she ain't never coming in our house.' He talks like that, 'ain't' and 'shi..it,' even though he's got a Ph.D. and a voice like a radio announcer; he was on the radio once and can speak as good as anybody. When I chide him, he'll say 'I's down home now chile. Jus' plain folks.' But that's his gift, to be an academic and to be just plain folks.

The words came pouring out of her, seemingly with no end and no beginning unless, "I'm so sorry," counted for the start.

"Peri," I began.

"Peri. Is that her name? That's very pretty. I imagine she's a very pretty girl. She'd have to be for you to like her. She's Governor Mattox's niece of course, that's why Al doesn't like her."

"Mattox?"

"Axe-handle Mattox. He used to be governor... for one term. All the white trash voted for him. Because he stood at the door of his restaurant with an axe-handle and wouldn't let Negroes in.

"I call them Negroes," she said when she saw the odd expression on my face, "sometimes, I'll call Al a nigger. That makes him mad. I say, 'you let other people call you nigger. People from school.'

"'That's different,' he'll reply, 'they're black.'

"'I'm black, too,' I'll answer, 'at least I'm married to a black man and I've got black children.' Well, black and white anyway. Though Kevin's more white than black and Daniel is as black as his Dad.

"I don't know why I married him. It seemed so simple at the time. Back in Ohio.

"Negroes weren't any different from us, I thought. They just had different colored skin and different, stronger features.

"Al was very handsome. He still is. He was the handsomest man I'd ever seen. Big and tall. I'm big and tall, too, have you noticed? Of course, a lot of girls are big and tall today, but not many were when I was growing up.

"Al was the captain of the football team, the defensive captain. And he was in a fraternity, a white fraternity. He had a great sense of humor and a big powerful laugh: you could hear his laugh two buildings away where my sorority was.

"He was the first man I ever made love to. I thought all men were like him. My parents, my liberal parents, didn't even want to meet him the first time they came to campus. 'We came to see you honey,' they said, butter melting from my mother's mouth, 'we came to spend time with you.' The next time they visited me and the next, Al was still there; they saw, finally, he wasn't going to go away, that I wasn't going to let him go away.

"He started graduate school in Agriculture at Ohio State; he was going to teach; I don't think we ever dreamed he'd get a doctorate. And I had another two years to go.

"We got married so we could live together in the married students' quarters and because my parents offered to support us if we did. I could have stayed in school and finished my degree—I was going to teach, too—but I got pregnant and I got pregnant again.

"Al has always been very good to me.

"He's very kind and very tender, even though he can be very rough with other people. I know he can be really rough on the people who work for him. Once, the Vu's were visiting us—she's that darling little Vietnamese lady; they escaped together, don't you know, from Vietnam in a tiny, little boat, though Mr. Vu wasn't her husband, then. Anyhow, a lot of people came over that day; Al was drinking heavily and wasn't really paying attention to any of them. He'd usually announce a party and then leave all the details to me, as if I didn't have enough on my hands with four kids, the three boys each as stubborn as their Dad.

"Anyhow, Al's out on the lawn drinking with one or two of his buddies, and I'm in the house trying to make everything go smoothly and explaining to Tinna that, no, she can't spend the night at Katisha's house, when I find Mrs. Vu all by herself in the bathroom. She's obviously been crying even though she says she hasn't, and then she starts crying again.

"'It's my husband,' she says, 'he's very depressed because your husband doesn't like him.' And then I have to explain for the one-thousandth time that Al does like Mr. Vu—I know, because he's told me what a find Mr. Vu is, but that he's rough because that's the way Al is. And all this while, Mrs. Vu is looking at me, and I know what she is thinking is the same thing that everyone else is thinking when they look at me, which is, she's so beautiful and yet her husband plays around.

"I'm sure he must have put the moves on Mrs. Vu too, maybe squeezed her little tit—did I shock you by saying that—and this is the real reason she's crying.

"I know he cheats on me. And it's not because I'm white, which is what some people say. Al cheats because all black men cheat on their wives; it's what they've been taught to do. They think cheating is part of what makes a man a man.

"He was better in Ohio, a little better, though he was cheating on me even back then. But back then, he felt guilty about it, while here, the other good old boys and those black single bitches that flounce around campus have convinced him it's the right thing to do.

"Miss Feret?" I ventured.

"Of course, he's screwed her, who hasn't? Won't help him though. That white fraternity he was so proud of getting into back at Ohio State? You know the fraternity is part of his problem?"

"What do you mean?" My throat was dry; I hadn't spoken in a long while and my voice sounded strange even to me.

"He was a Beta back at Ohio State; he thought that was really great then, the first black in an all-white fraternity. But all the important people on campus, President Benjamin, Beau-Beau Lee, Mr. Nathaniel, all the other Deans belong to Alpha Chi. Alpha was blacks-only back when blacks couldn't belong to any other kind of fraternity, and it's blacks-only still because that is the way the blacks want it to be. No whites and no blacks with white wives like my husband need apply."

I spoke again. I had no choice. "Alpha Chi is the fraternity Steve Marshall was pledging, isn't it?"

"The boy who drowned. You won't let it alone, will you? Al was sort of amused that you wouldn't let it alone. It was driving all the other Deans mad. They were so busy hushing it up. 'That boy's going to get hi' self in trouble,' he'd say about you in his fake down-home accent.

"'Won't you help Dr. Wood, Al,' I asked him once, 'for me.'

"'Not while he lives with that white trash bitch.'

"I'm sorry, that's what Al said. I'm sure Peri is a very wonderful girl. Peri, that's what you said her name was?"

I nodded once more, my neck stiff and sore as if I'd been holding it against possible attack. We'd let the hot spring day decay around us. The neon signs had come on now and dusk had given way to dark. Across the highway, the words "Motel, vacancy" winked on and off. Maybe it was time we went inside the bar and had that drink she'd talked about.

I turned sideways on the seat toward her and found she was looking directly at me in a hungry, almost predatory fashion. The vacant stare was gone. Somehow she'd succeeded in purging herself of all her ghosts, while my own troubles were still active and alive.

"Will you make love to me?" Her voice was soft; the words unexpected.

Our hands touched, then her lips were on mine, her body pressed against me. The seat back gave away suddenly, a cause for laughter; instead, she continued to cling to me; she cupped my rear with one hand, pressed the full-length of her body against mine.

Across the highway, the slot outside vacant cabin number nine waited for our car. "I'll pay," she said.

The rooms were not designed for long stays; the single queen-size bed sagged in the middle, its greasy bedspread heavy with dust. We could hear the shower drip-dripping in the background.

"Take your clothes off," she said. She did not hesitate an instant before removing her own clothing. Her large breasts bounced in front of me as she took off blouse and bra in a single sweeping motion.

Her body was the Playmate of my fantasies. Large perfectly formed breasts that perhaps were as firm as the day Al first held them in his hands, though now the nipples were much longer, their owner trained to respond to a suck with tiny gasps, to beg "put it in me, put it in me," and cup my ass in her hands, forcing, when I still wanted to explore her hips and thighs, rain kisses on those massive buttocks.

To keep from coming once I was inside, I had to push the image of her beauty away, impose a list of bones—ilium, ischium, pubis, and a second list of thigh muscles—ilipsoas, pectineus, rectus femoris, adductor longus, but it was too late, her firm body gripped my penis and I was gone, cum inside her, asleep and left alone to wake, take my shower—only the one damp towel remained for my use, then creep back across the highway.

We had a new housemate when I returned to Pineville that night.

"Who is she?" I asked Peri, referring to the young girl who was stretched out on the couch in the front room. She couldn't have been more than 13 or 14. Another grandchild?

"She'll be staying with us for a few days," was all I got from Peri in the girl's presence, but early the next morning, when the almost-anorexic teen had been packed off to school with a lunch Peri had made for her, when Peri saw I didn't intend to leave for work until I had the whole, the complete story, she told me about the girl.

Kim lived around the corner. (I though I'd seen her before.) She'd been seeing a boy her parents thought was unsuitable. (Why? "He's black." Heavens to Murgatroyd.) They hadn't been dating—her parents still didn't allow her to date, but she'd been seeing the boy every chance she could get after school and in school between classes.

"I'm sure you know who she is." Peri said, "You must have recognized her. (Where? when?)

"You saw them together one or two times yourself." Where? "The woods near the park, where you know, you and I go sometimes." And we did go, had gone, particularly in the heat that previous fall, gone to find coolness and a quiet place, gone to be together. I could visualize this other couple now, two teenagers, one black, one white, fingers touching, not quite holding hands, briefly glimpsed through the trees.

Their proximity at school was how the problem had begun. The school principal, noticing the two were constantly together or having his attention drawn to their closeness by one of the more conscientious school employees, had telephoned the girl's father, (stepfather, Peri corrected) and told him. But why, I asked, why did the principal get involved? "He didn't want the man to think the school was behind it."

"And step dad went through the roof," I said.

"Dad and Mom and everybody. They told her to stop seeing the boy, and Kim said, O.K., figuring she'd get around them somehow. Then her parents announced they were moving to Florida—they were smart enough to realize that moving was the only way they could get her to keep her promise. So that was when Kim ran away. To here."

"Around the block." I said, amused.

"It's better she stay with us, then live on the streets." Peri's harsh tone warned me she would not have her judgments mocked.

"A lot better. You did the right thing," I said, responding to her tone.

"Thanks. I wanted you to say that."

I was holding Peri, trying to prove to her we were still one, when the doorbell rang.

The early-morning caller was Kim's father, stepfather. "My daughter here?" he asked belligerently.

"Sh.. . she's at school." No reason for me to stammer, but I was facing one angry man.

"You that professor fellow?"

I nodded.

"Teach at the colored school? You like them colored do you?"

"Not particularly."

"What?!" (He hadn't expected that answer.)

"I like some of them; I don't like others. Most of the blacks we have at Benjamin aren't very good students. A few, a very few, though, are outstanding, and good friends of mine, I hope. A couple of the black profs are sharp, but most are crocs. Why else would they be at Benjamin?"

Kim's Dad looked dazed, even bored by my garrulousness, but I, too, was angry, with something I needed to get off my mind.

"Most of the Benjamin administrators are crafty, back-stabbing bastards that I wouldn't tell the time to for fear they'd steal my watch. But one person I work for, a black woman, the Vice-President for Long Range Planning, is someone I'd follow anywhere. She's like my thesis advisor, just one of the best, the greatest people there is."

"My daughter," he said. He seemed out of words though it was I who had been doing all of the talking.

I said, "I'll have her call you when she gets back from school. Maybe you guys can sit down and work something out."

"It's worth a try." he replied and shrugged. "Not much you can do when they get this way though. Moving may be the only thing we can do."

He looked up at the sky for a moment where a sliver of a moon could be seen just above the horizon. "You got daughters?" he asked.

"Yeah, three. Two almost grown and one who thinks she is." I smiled.

"It's hell ain't it?" He smiled back.

"You'd better believe it."

We parted friends. Peri agreed to have the girl telephone her parents when she got back from school. "Be sure to tell her she can still stay with us," I added and drove off to Fort Lee and the campus where everybody hated me.

Chapter 28.

I didn't hear any more about being fired for the next week or so, but that didn't mean the process wasn't grinding on in the background. I wasn't sure just how the actual termination would come, a letter in the mail? Or all the administrators in the President's office, a big room, the President behind his desk, Dean Holley's face turned from me, Beau-Beau Lee's face savage, Mr. Nathaniel handing me the envelope, a form to sign, turn in your key?

I visited an attorney. Yes, he knew about the college, was suing them on behalf of someone else. That's how I know about you, I told him, the "someone else" had recommended him. But my case was different, he interrupted, I hadn't been at Benjamin long enough to qualify. Still, I should gather evidence, observe, take notes during conversations. Perhaps, something in my complaints about the chemistry laboratory, some statute that protected whistle-blowers might be applicable.

As usual, I had too much to do at school to worry about my next step; barely enough hours existed in each working day in which to do what had to be done now.

I had a new assessment program to set up and supervise in addition to all the standard minutiae of my working day. Raymond White's attendance had been irregular; sometimes he would phone in and cancel a class, sometimes he would not bother to call and I knew only because Ernestine would appear outside my office door and behind her, a pack of disgruntled students.

Was I fired or wasn't I? My contract said three years. Yes, said my attorney, but his finger pointed to the words, "to be renewed on an annual basis."

Mr. Nathaniel, the evil figure of my waking dream could probably have told me the answer. This novel would have been more interesting had I been able to follow him from place to place.

Did he meet with senior members of his fraternity on weekends, other tall, elegant black men like himself? Or did he simply reach his decision over coffee in the Benjamin cafeteria, a chance conversation with a former coworker, the bookstore lady, the head of the athletic department, the ones he'd risen above in power and title but never in spirit?

Did my error lay in attacking fraternities or in advocating change? my will opposed to those determined things would go on as before. The mind a terrible thing to waste.

He was standing outside the bookstore, a lit cigarette in his hand, relaxing and, for once, free of sycophantic hangers-on. I stopped near him and tried to look amiable.

He was a very tall man, even bent over, half-crouched, shielding his cigarette from the wind, his face was still several inches above mine. "I think we can put through that order for a safety shower, now," he said, scrapping the ashes from his cigarette with a stained yellow fingernail.

"I just have to balance things." he continued, not really talking to me, but to some unseen persons offstage. "I've had that responsibility for a long, long time.

"There weren't but three or four buildings here to begin with. Not air-conditioned, not heated in the winter or cooled in the summer. We actually had to provide our own stoves that first year. Then, I don't know, when the State wouldn't install any, they persuaded Mr. Parsons to donate a couple of his company's old stoves. Not good enough for his workers but good enough for a black college.

"Budget didn't go very far then, doesn't go very far now.

"We don't even get to keep the fees, did you know that? You think you're successful, raising enrollments, attracting new students."

Startled by the sudden reference to my program, and forgetting my promise to be cool and attentive to my superiors, I blurted out, "But President Benjamin said..."

"Shit on that. Your success has cost us a fortune. Our budget is set by the State two years in advance. Attract more students as you did, make the courses too popular, it costs us just as much money as if not enough students were to show up. The State's given us what they figure we need and they're not going to give us a penny more."

He looked off in the distance again. A few students and teachers strode by in the break between classes, but they gave us a wide berth.

"We were going to go under in '74. 'What can we do?' Dr. Henderson asked me; he was the President, then. And a good man, too. He was our kind; him, I didn't mind helping; he believed. I picked up the phone, I called people I knew, people I'd gone to school with, 'can you get us money?' I asked.

"They said, 'maybe,' they didn't say yes, didn't make promises they couldn't keep. But all of a sudden, ads appeared on television, 'help the black colleges.' Money came in from Washington, first one grant then another. Up in Atlanta, they decided maybe they ought to send us some money, too."

He paused; a terrible weariness seemed to have settled upon him, upon both of us. "The people I called may not have had much money themselves, that's why you don't see any big buildings here named after some black billionaire, but they did have connections, they did know people who could get things done.

"Now, you come along and you want to change things. Maybe what you say will work and that would be good. But you know, I get to thinking you don't plan to stay around to see if your ideas do work. You come here with your nose in the air figuring we' were nigger trash; you was goin t'do yo' thing, and talk your talk, and then let Mr. Nathaniel figure out how to keep it all going, once you were gone and the novelty wore off."

He leaned toward me like a giraffe bending to touch its young, his lips close to my ear. "Well, this College will keep going long after you're gone, long after President Benjamin has worn through his last vest, long after I'm buried and in the ground."

I knew then he was as dedicated as I, and that when the time came to fire me, he would give no more thought to me and my ambitions than I had given to the Singhs and Mr. Sun. I was a legend only in my own mind.

The last three or four times I'd been fired, I'd really had nothing to lose. Oh, the money, but that was replaceable. Now I had something, someone, Peri.

Would she stay with me? At the height of our happiness, just back from the Bahamas, she'd told me it wouldn't last. I'd purchased her favor while I had a job with a salary large by local standards. If I left Georgia for California, tail between my legs, what chance that she would follow?

Chapter 29.

"But what about the students?" my oldest daughter Samantha asked.

More and more, with no outlet for my doubts but the lining of my duodenum, I had taken to calling one or the other of my daughters and recounting the latest of the day's intrigues.

"Before you went to Benjamin," Samantha continued, "all you could talk about were your plans for revolutionizing the curriculum, teaching the students to think, teaching them to create, to be the best that they could be. But you don't talk about the students anymore. Instead, it's the Dean this and the Vice-President that and what Achmed said and is Merrill Jefferson really your friend or your enemy? What happened to your vision?"

I'm fighting to survive, I thought, but I didn't say that aloud. A father wants to be a hero to his children.

Maybe, my pretense at heroism, my ongoing self-deception had been the problem from the beginning. Instead of 'fessing up and admitting this job at Benjamin was the best I could do at this stage of my wasted career, I'd turned Benjamin into a quest, cast myself as a Sir Galahad bent on righting wrongs and doing good. "And you can't do that and survive," the deep voice of the Dean, now part of my own personality, said inside.

I visited the Science building that weekend, ostensibly to gather documentation for my forthcoming lawsuit. Truthfully, it was more of an attempt to recall and experience happier times.

The campus was deserted. Long gleaming corridors echoed with my footsteps. Monday would see the returned hordes, but that night, no one was there to hear me, no one to acknowledge their Captain's presence at the classroom door, shy smiles from the students, their instructor looking up from his notes to see Professor Wood.

A wave of my hand to an invisible class and I walk on down the hall. On the third floor, where the chemistry laboratory is located, a single light spills out across the corridor from an open door.

I found White alone in his office, staring at the walls. "How's it going?" I said.

He didn't look up at first; I guess his mind was elsewhere, like mine, wandering up and down long empty corridors. "It's all meaningless," he shouted, though not at me, at the walls, or at someone beyond the walls, another prisoner, perhaps.

Most of the reverberations were inside him. I could see it pained him to tell me, to tell himself that his life no longer mattered.

"I'm not very good," he said, "always thought I could be someone important like my mama wanted me to be, another George Washington Carver. But agronomy was too simple—yesterday's headlines. DNA stuff seemed too risky. I did Paramecia instead. Found myself a nice white liberal who thought blacks deserved a break—four generations of slavery, you know. Paramecia were his thing—how'd I know, dumb black boy, that no one gives a shit about Paramecia. Three years wasted. Guy down the hall did DNA. Spent all his time fixing the sequencer; still there when I left. Never did get his Ph.D., either, but you know, he's got his own damn company."

Ron, Ronald, sat back heavily in his chair, his hams making a splat against the hard wooden surface. "I've been where you are," he said, though he was not staring at me but through me, "They take you in; they use you up. Knew I didn't have a Ph.D., but said they wanted someone to fill the gap. State pays them for the doctorate just as if I really had one.

"Looks good, too, to see a brother as a chairperson." Hands interlaced behind his head, he looked up at me, at me, not though me, for the first time. "You ain't a brother."

He eyed my clothes. Ran his fingers to the ends of his own sharp lapels. Looked at me again and shook his head in wonder. "Shit man, you look like you just came off the fuck'n golf course."

No one here to impress, no one besides me to wonder how he kept his suit so wrinkle free. Not a spot of dandruff on his shoulders, not a speck of lint.

What was he wearing a suit for?

"'Course, when you and I wear lab coats, we both look the same."

Not true. My lab coat was two sizes too large; it fit my shoulders, just, but swallowed my torso like a boy's. Was it his build?

"Christ." He sighed as if reading my thoughts. "You can order lab coats like mine through the Paras Catalog. Here." He rummaged briefly in his desk, then tossed a rolled up form to me. "You the chairman and assistant dean, let the school pay for your clothes.

"You know why they're not having you back?"

He had switched topics, again, first from his personal despair to my appearance and now to the core, to the nitty gritty, to where it was at, down and dirty.

My lips were dry. I did and did not want to hear what he would tell me. But for an instant, something in our mutual glances was almost akin to love.

He shook his head slowly back and forth as if doubting in advance my ability to understand what he would say. "You don' dress the part. You don' act the part. Professor, Chairman, Assistant Dean suppos' t'be something special. You ordinary. Man, I 'spect someday you come to school without shoes."

How could he know how much I liked to walk Huck feet in the dust, in Quaker gray, dressed down and simple? And does simple dress make a difference that inner voice chided, when a man is so puffed up within?

"Shit, let's go play some pool."

He stood up, shot his cuffs, and smoothed an invisible wrinkle from his suit coat. I followed him blindly along the corridor, down the stairs, and to his car.

The Mercedes' engine didn't make a sound. When I cracked a window, he looked at me oddly. For him, it was automatic to roll up the windows, turn on the air-conditioning. But I liked the smell of the Georgia night, savored the mixture of down-home cooking mixed with pine and pecan.

We left the main streets. I didn't know where we were going, realized I probably didn't want to know, let my head fall against the leather upholstery, welcomed the knowledge that someone else was in control.

A row of mostly-occupied parking slots filled the narrow alley that separated our destination from the adjacent building. The pungent smell of vinegary barbecue, stale beer and a gym's worth of stale sweat greeted us at the door.

He stopped in the doorway for a moment till he was sure he had my attention, touched his fingers to his lips, then ushered me ahead of him into the bar.

"Hey Ron," "Ronald MacDonald," smiling white teeth greet us from the shadows that gather along the edges of the brightly lit pool tables. He bows; I follow inconspicuously, my eyes roaming like a cop's, no one else's eyes ever really meeting mine.

"You got money, Ronald?"

"I play for ribs. Eightball. My frien' and I be partners."

"The Good Doctor," I heard someone say. A student? No. My reputation had preceded me. To wherever we were.

"Break," Ronald said to me.

I selected a cue. When had I played last? The student union at Berkeley? No, when I was working in San Diego for Jim and Bud. Long lunches, eight ball after and sometimes before and during. I broke nicely, balls spreading evenly about the table, sank a stripe. Sank another stripe. Missed a long shot completely. About par for me. Chuckles round the table. Every face was black, didn't give a damn. Ronald's voice in my ear, "Don't do this professionally." Ronald's voice aloud, "I can taste those ribs."

"Shit." And our skinny opponent scratched.

Someone put a beer in my hand, a Budweiser, no chance to ask for Sharps non-alcoholic. Ronald put away four balls. So did our deep-voiced roly-poly opponent with the glasses. Doc they called him. "Three doctors at the table." "He cuts hair," Ronald whispered in my ear, "An' you know 'bout me."

I sank the easy one Doc had left me. Lucked out on a shot across the table, barely missed scratching. Someone offered to show me how to bank one out of the corner. Ronald said, "The Good Doctor know what he doing," and then proceeded to show me how to make the shot.

I grazed the ball I was aiming for; no one was impressed. But we got the ribs anyway when skinny sank the eight.

"We hears you hard on the students," skinny said when we were standing at the bar, ribs in one hand, beer in the other. I smiled, beamed, mouth crammed with rib and slaw, said nothing, remembered Ronald's warning at the door.

Ronald spoke for me, "Dr. Wood change things around. Benjamin tough as Harvard now, tough as Georgia Tech."

"Shit." went the cries around the table, but the point had been made, and as my eyes adjusted to the dimness, I saw a table full of Benjamin students in the corner, pride filled, straightening, slowly realizing they were part of this new image. Pity I wouldn't be back to see it.

Chapter 30.

I had another telephone call from my oldest daughter. This time she suggested I write a book, about working at a black college and having three daughters. With flashbacks, I suppose, to a time when I actually had three daughters whom I kissed in the morning before they went to school and kissed at night before they went to bed, or, if I got home late, kissed as I went tiptoeing from bedroom to bedroom tucking them in.

I've written a book, I told her. In my spare time. In someone else's office, at a borrowed desk. *Permutation Tests*. The subtitle is 'Resampling Methods for Testing Hypotheses in Biology and Medicine.'

"That's a statistics text, Dad. Why don't you write one about people?"

"I don't understand people very well."

"Maybe the book wlll help."

The kid was right as always: I needed that book.

When I got home from school that night, I told Peri just the way it had happened. Beau-Beau Lee's office, Mr. Nathaniel standing on the side, some lady I'd never met from personnel. My Dean was not there; they told me later he didn't even know it was going to happen, it had shaken him up a little when he heard the news. The Dean and I had spent the morning reviewing the budget and the curriculum for the following year. "Type it up," he'd said. The note on my desk read, "See Beau-beau Lee." Ernestine was not at her desk.

Midway through the firing, Beau-Beau Lee got so angry he forgot his lines. Nathaniel leaned forward, pointed to a sheet of paper on Beau-Beau's desk, and when Beau-Beau still did not understand, underlined three of the items in red for him. "Failure to cooperate with other members of the faculty," "Errors in attendance records," "Repeated need for administrative counseling."

"So you see, Mr. Wood," the lady from personnel said, "We could terminate you right now, but with only a few weeks left in the term, we thought..."

Dr. Wood," I corrected.

Though I told my story to Peri only once, by the time I was through telling it, I felt that I'd repeated it again and again to an unfeeling audience, a detached interrogator who would want it repeated one more time. I don't know what I expected, an outpouring of sympathy or shared anger, but not this impersonal detachment.

She kept her arms folded across her chest, throughout, her expression unchanging. When I was finished, she got up from the table still without speaking, and began to carry the dishes back into the kitchen. I followed, arms loaded, and hovered in the background, while she fussed at the sink, her back to me.

I told her we'd go forward. Back to California. I'd find another job. Lots to do in California, I said,

"You never take me anyplace," she began unexpectedly.

"We go dancing almost every weekend!"

"We go dancing because you want to go dancing. And you dance with other girls, you don't just dance with me. We go to movies that you want to see." she continued.

"I thought we had fun doing things together."

She hit the cupboard with her hand. Water shot from her hands to the counter; she wiped at the damp spots for an instant, then threw the dishtowel into a corner. "Just once, I wish you would take me somewhere and do something because I want to do it, not because you thought it would be fun. I can make my own decisions."

My shoulders tensed; I locked my hands and pitted the two sides of my body against one other in a test of strength. Peri, if you only remembered how many things I've done with you, for you, done simply because they gave you pleasure, because I wanted to be with you.

Suddenly, her hand appeared in front of my face, waving frantically. "I'm angry," she said.

Why had she turned on me?

"You've tuned me out."

"I'm listening."

"You don't listen. You don't even let me complete my sentences. All you really care about is you."

I stammered, tried to interrupt, to understand.

"I'm supposed to be your girl, but when we meet another woman, you run your eyes up and down her body. Jewel tells me that once when you two were alone, you tried to put the moves on her."

Jewel? I needed Peri's support, her sympathy. Not this. I had just lost my job. I needed Peri to help me work it out, to be together.

"And what about you and Jewel?" I said. "Fucking dyke."

I saw the movement, the blur of her hand. Then my eyes filled with tears as the sting turned into a slap that rocked me back. By the time I looked up, Peri had disappeared into the bedroom.

I wish I could say I rushed after her, apologized, tried to explain, said, "I'm sorry," but instead I repeated the words "fucking dyke" over and over softly to myself and wished her gone.

I did not apologize later when she emerged from the bedroom, a suitcase in her hand.

"Where are you going?"

She dodged out of reach and walked straight across the room to the front door. There, she turned to look at me, her head cocked on one side like a beseeching bird. I put on my best sneer. I wouldn't say anything, wouldn't give her the satisfaction.

She had to get in the last word. "Peter, that was a rotten thing for you to say. About her. Not about me, about her. If you can't tell that I love you, if you don't know what I'm like, then you don't love me."

I opened my mouth. To defend myself? to apologize?

"No, don't try to tell me that you love me, it's too late. I'm going." And she stomped out, suitcase in hand, leaving me alone in her house with the bedspread that smelled of her, bureau drawers still packed with her things, the mixed scent of sandalwood and potpourri, left me alone to stew, to anger, to feel sorry for myself.

Chapter 31.

Don't think I was always walking up and down the street where she'd moved in with Jewel, a bouquet of flowers in my hand, suffering, longing, too timid to knock, too angry.

Or that an indecisive hour later, the stems crushed, flowers wilted, I rush faster and faster into the gathering darkness, past Jewel's house one final time, past Kim's two blocks over, past our own tiny cottage, to the park where we'd walked together each evening, where other lovers still walked in pairs.

Too many evenings, I simply stayed curled up on the couch, depressed, useless, wondering where I would go next. I could not stay, a foreigner in the South, could not, would not without her beside me.

Do not believe I fought the depression. I gave way to it, cursed Peri for leaving me alone. Am I the source of my undoing, sad and angry, a burden to myself? Then let me curse my God and die.

And yet, the last verses of Jonah say—where's my Bible (Peri has one, leather bound, she takes to church each Sunday. Peri!)

"And it came to pass
When the sun arose
That God prepared a vehement East wind
And the sun so beat upon the head of Jonah
that he fainted
and requested for himself, that he might die
and said 'It is better for me to die, than to live.'

God said to Jonah,
'Art thou greatly angry for the gourd.'
Jonah said, 'I am greatly angry, even unto death.'

The Lord said, 'Thou hast had pity on the gourd,
for which thou neither labored, nor maddest it grow
which came up in a night
and perished in a night.

And should not I have pity on Ninevah,
that great city,
wherein are more than six score thousand persons
that cannot discern between their right hand
and their left hand, and also much cattle?'"

I waited a day, two days before I realized, I could not, did not want to live without her. During the day, I could always find something to do with myself. Masturbate, tinker with the car, send out job applications. But weekend or weekday, by evening following a too-early supper, the loneliness would set in. Stay out of the bedroom, all her clothes are there; her dresses hang in the closet; her sweaters are neatly folded in the cedar chest at the foot of the bed.

I hold a sweater to my nostrils, smell it, place it back. Surely she'll need some of her clothing. Will come back one evening to pick some up.

And when she did not come and did not come, I stopped finally outside the small brown two-story wood framed house on Mulberry where Jewel lived, where Peri lived with her, where I still did not believe the things people said the two of them did together.

A hard driving disco beat, the same music Jewel played at aerobics in the gym, spilled down across the lawn to the sidewalk where I lurked, frozen, trying to see, to hear, to know what went on inside.

I dragged myself, a reluctant spy, up onto the porch and peeked through their living room curtains. Soft muted tones, a leather couch, Navajo blanket on the floor. A Nordic Track apparatus next to the stereo. Books, a very few of them, near a glass coffee table with an open magazine, Peri's habit, nearby on the floor. No one in the room.

The music came from the room beyond. I stepped back quickly from the window, afraid they'd see me, afraid I'd catch them unprepared. I waited, heard the music, knocked, then pounded on Jewel's front door.

The handle turned, Peri appeared in the opening, barefoot in shorts. Her nipples, enormous and distended, stood out plainly against the material of her thin gray sweater. I had an instant erection, diminished a moment later by the appearance of Jewel, gray-haired, drab in a shapeless t-shirt, hovering just behind her.

Peri turned, her face on a level with Jewel's shoulder, her eyes invisible to me. "I'll speak to him alone," she said to Jewel. "Yes?" she continued, turning back.

"Come home," I said.

"When you move out. No, you don't have to move out now," she continued when she saw my stricken look, "I know you have another week or so of school. But when the vacation starts; you'll have to find a new place, somewhere you can live next year."

"I don't think there'll be a next year."

Concern, doubt, fondness, distrust of me flickered one after the other across her face. "No," she said, her tone serious and thoughtful, "I'm sure they mean to keep you on."

For a moment, I thought I saw her tremble; I reached out a hand to steady, to reassure her, to make myself and the love we'd shared felt a second time.

Jewel's head appeared again over Peri's shoulder, "Why don't you invite him inside?"

Bitch.

"Jewel," Peri said firmly, "I told you I wanted to talk to Peter alone. Now, this is your house and I can't tell you what to do in it, so Peter and I will go for a walk. Is that all right Peter?"

I nodded helpless, though oddly, at that instant I felt far from helpless, even exultant. Maybe, I had a chance after all.

"No, Peter, there's no chance." she said as we walked along arm and arm. "But I am fond of you and I don't want to see you being hurt. Or your daughters either. I know you need the money to send to them."

"If you were to come back..." I began.

"Peter, I'm not coming back."

My face showed that I knew, was prepared to accept what she was telling me. I wasn't, of course.

"I bought you flowers." I said, "I don't have them with me now. I'll bring you them by, later."

For an instant, a dreamy smile played across her face, and then she shook her head. "I'm going to go back in the house, now. Thank you for coming. Bye."

I stared at her beseeching, trying to hold her with my eyes. I could feel myself reaching out for her, but found nothing, nothing in return. "Kiss me," I begged.

She reached up and kissed me on the lips, keeping her body and her nipples at a distance. Then she walked away.

Chapter 32.

The end of each college year is marked by a ceremony of passage: Commencement, graduation. Some look back in anger, some—the increasing numbers of Generation X students without jobs or prospects—ahead in fear. A very, very few look all around with awareness. I was not among them.

Though I was due to depart the college permanently only a few weeks later, Merrill Jefferson insisted it was my duty to attend. "These are your students,"—they had been in my charge for only a year—"they've worked hard,"—a patent lie for some, an exaggeration for the majority—"they must be able to rely on you to acknowledge their efforts."

So I went to graduation, for love of Merrill and, perhaps, a sneaking affection for one or two of the students—Martin King, Delores, Val Haxtun, Katisha—who had been kind to me.

The graduation ceremonies promised to be a hard, difficult three hours. President Benjamin would speak. So would Beau-Beau Lee, far too long as always. We'd hear the battered diction of one or two valedictorians, plus a half dozen other familiar faces, already too often seen.

The Lt. Governor of Georgia would speak, so would the Mayor of Atlanta. Both would receive honorary degrees. Outstanding students would be recognized along with alumni of little distinction; Steven Marshall would lay forgotten despite all his father's best efforts.

In the parking lot outside my office I sprinkled the rim of a plastic champagne glass with salt before filling it with Jose Cuevero from my thermos. A second baggie provided slices of lemon for the quintessential Margarita.

The first glassful I used to quench my thirst. Rolling down the car window—no point leaving it up once I'd turned off the air-conditioning, I savored the second. I poured a third glass, then climbed unsteadily from the car, turning gradually east by northeast so that I faced toward the college. Curving lines of the black-garbed penitent led the way to the quadrangle, where I let Merrill and Professor B guide me to my seat.

"You've got to get rid of that," Merrill whispered, pointing to my glass. And so I did. Drank it down like a good soldier, crushed the plastic and hid it inside my gown, letting the warm glow of tequila radiate freely throughout my head and body.

I rose when told to applaud, sat still otherwise, laughed often, though I seldom got the jokes, sat serious and somber when the crowd did likewise and was the very best of companions. I swear I'll miss those fellows.

Afterward, I was sober enough, I think, to shake Martin King's hand and meet his mom and dad. Kermie hadn't come to graduation. Pity, I'd have liked to meet his family, tell them how much I admired their son.

I was sober and alert (almost) by the time I reached the parking lot, sober enough to drive, alert enough to realize that what had happened was not some grand epiphany, the final

Chapter of some absurd academic novel, but simply another episode in the life of a sad and angry man.

Did it matter whether my contract was canceled or extended? I would find another job, though perhaps still not the one my talents sought. Life with Peri was not so easily surrendered. She had meant little to me when I started, another town, another dame. She was my life now. Oh Peri, come back to me.

I was still filled with love and brotherhood for all mankind, when, final drive from Fort Lee completed, I tumbled into her little cottage.

Peri was sitting on the living room couch in a room barely brightened by the still-setting sun. "You're drunk," she said, though I'd not had a drop for more than four hours.

"I'm happy," I said.

"You're happy then," and, unexpectedly, she kissed me. "And you stink of tequila." But I did not reply for I was already asleep in her arms.

I woke in the middle of the night. Hot and sticky, and still no rain. "I love you Peri," I said, and rolled over in bed, suddenly afraid. No, she was still there next to me, wearing only a thin half-negligee. A wisp of her blond hair had fallen down over her cheek and, still asleep, a slim hand reached up and brushed at it. I cried hot sticky tears of joy. Then, I kissed her cheek, put my arms about her and held her close. “I love you Peri,” I whispered. She did not reply, but her hips began to move against mine.

Chapter 33.

In the morning, we made love again. I heated the water for coffee; she fixed eggs and bacon. Fed, rested, delirious with her perfume, the smell of her body, the tang of her nether lips, I could tell her my plan:

We'd go to California. Together. I'd look for a job; we'd be near my kids; she wouldn't have to worry about working, could surf with me on the weekends, garden all-year round in the desert sun.

But I didn't voice any of these thoughts aloud. She wouldn't, couldn't go with me. She had children of her own here, too many ties, no reason to trust, yet, that I would live up to my promises.

A man named Hussein Chung, not a psychologist, just a very wise man, taught me when I couldn't solve a problem by myself, too many self-deceptions impeding the way, to share it with others, to get all aspects of the problem, even and especially the hard-to-confess ones, out in the open. I would be pitied, perhaps, scorned, perhaps, but, in the end, understood.

I didn't have all the answers, so I shared my dilemma with Peri, the woman I loved, trusted, and, I felt, cared a very great deal for me. She heard me out, touched my cheek with her tiny hand. "Stay at Benjamin. You could be Dean," she said.

I didn't tell her how afraid I was of going back to the college, how in the last weeks I'd begun to park my car at a distance for fear some disgruntled student would slash my tires. Or that more and more of my colleagues, told I threatened their livelihood, had turned their backs on me.

"I'll give it a try." I said.

It's no good trying to understand the South. Who knows what hidden wires linked my blond rural paramour to a man as thoroughly urbanized and black as Samuel Benjamin. But he returned my phone calls, finally, and granted me a face-to-face in his office. We were not alone. Mr. Nathaniel was an awesome presence in the background. Beau-Beau Lee, the Vice-President for academic affairs and Thomas Holley, my Dean, were there, too. I got to speak my piece, and describe all I'd accomplished for the good of the college. Beau-Beau and Dean Holley got to speak theirs and describe all I'd done wrong. The President said he'd heard good things about me. Nathaniel, speaking in my presence for perhaps only the second time, said yes, he too had heard good things, but left off in a manner that suggested he'd heard the bad things, too.

"About the drowning," I began.

"What has poor Steven's death got to do with it?" roared the Dean.

"Why everything. You know perfectly well he was killed in a hazing incident and my termination is only incidental to the cover up."

Cries of outrage filled the room.

"You have no proof," Nathaniel said.

"It's not really a question of proof but of what Steven's father wants to believe," I retorted, stopping them all as effectively as a pail of water had stopped the Wicked Witch of the East.

"I've made a decision," said the President. "The Professor is too good a scholar; we can't afford to lose him. He's done good things with his community relations program, and the students, those who don't hate him, tell me he's gotten them jobs."

"Let's hope they keep them," Beau-Beau interjected, but the President chose not to hear.

"I think we're just overworking the poor man. Let's get him out of the classroom and in a position to do those things he's so capable of doing."

Nathaniel smiled. Not a good sign. Beau-Beau and Dean Holley looked crestfallen, so perhaps they didn't understand the full measure of my promotion.

I'd been kept on, this was the good news I'd relay to Peri; I'd even been kicked upstairs where it would look better on my resume. But I was out of the day-to-day operations of the college, out of Nathaniel's hair.

In the end, the President's decision didn't make any difference, at least not as far as he himself was concerned. Darren Marshall, Steven's father, would not let the inquiry die. Someone had to be guilty and that someone proved to be President Benjamin, the man who'd given me back my job. He was replaced, rather too quickly, I thought, with an equally glib figurehead.

For I'd been wrong all along about Samuel Benjamin and Benjamin College, and my boss, Thomas Holley, had been right. Nathaniel and the Alpha Phi Alpha fraternity were the real powers; they'd been on hand when the college was called Black Teachers Institute; they would be there when the State finally renamed Benjamin the University of Georgia at Fort Lee.

I served out the following year (not the two additional years that had been contracted for), received glowing references, and Peri came with me to California bringing part of the red Georgia clay with her.

Despite California's own economic difficulties, we survive. I teach part time, have interviewed twice for a position as Dean, and once in a while I sell an article on education to a national magazine.

We go back to Georgia, together, at least once a year or she threatens to go alone. I go with her because I find I am not happy when she is out of my sight for even a short period. I see her bewildered, losing her way, wisp of blond hair over her eyes, though I know in truth she is indefatigable and enormously self-reliant. She was there for me when help was needed, consoling, comforting, not just in richness and health. She gave me backbone at a time my face was still buried in my hands.

Merrill was promoted to Dean this June. He has written asking if I would consider returning to head up the freshman-orientation program. I will share this letter with Peri when she comes home this evening.

Peri is a good and a dutiful wife. She has persuaded me to like and even to enjoy Southern cooking (though at my request, she has cut out the salt, and uses butter only sparingly). I trust her completely. But I hold her tight because I do not want to ever let her go.

Chapter 34.

"The important thing is you are now willing to admit that none of these events ever happened," Dr. W. says, "That Peri in particular is entirely a figment of imagination, someone you invented to tie you through a difficult period. The first year or so after your wife left, you knew you were incapable of forming a relationship, so you had Peri, an imaginary playmate. It's normal; it's healthy, that is, if you're willing to leave it behind and move on."

"My girlfriend left me." I am thinking of an event only a few weeks old, though Dr. W. has no way of knowing this.

"Your girlfriend, your wife, it does not matter. The important thing is that you are starting to get better."

"I don't think I'll ever forget her," I persist, striving for dramatic impact with my voice, but Dr. W does not rise to the bait. Still I wait several expensive moments before I return to the original topic.

"Mrs. Angel, Miss S., Ernestine. Do you believe they're real?"

"It doesn't matter what I believe, Peter, it matters what you believe. Mrs. Angel, I can believe, though whether she worked at the school or you just met her in a bar, I can't be sure. Sounds like transitory relationships were all you were capable of forming at the time. But again Peter, I insist that what is important at this instant in time is that you are able to recognize the distinction between what is real and what you just made up."

I don't care. I think I still miss her.

And again I remember our last night together, her hesitation, almost reluctance. I begin to stimulate her the way I always have, she gives herself up to my hands and when I drew her to me takes me willingly into her mouth, and later, when totally aroused, deep inside her, parting her thighs fully to a degree she'd never permitted before.

"Peter!"

My father's voice, peremptory, demanding

"Cat caught your tongue?" Dr W. asks.

"I was just thinking," I begin

"I know. But we agreed we would stay in the here and now during our sessions. Peter. You are well. You can remain well, or you can become the prisoner of your own thoughts. It's up to you."

I don't respond. I am a rock, an island. "The drowning was real."

"I'm sure it was."

"I read about it in the paper. The school gym, some sort of fraternity party."

"An accident, I gather."

"Perhaps, the circumstances were suspicious. I meant to investigate."

"But you didn't. Like all of us, you read about unnecessary tragedy, rant and rave about the cruelty of man, perhaps have a moment in which you think you might act, then put it aside, go on with your life—the paper boy is at the door collecting, the sheets need to be transferred from washer to dryer—that's normal, too. Don't blame yourself."

You don't understand, Dr. W. I want something far different than your cold analytic mind: a father's touch, cookies with raisins-in. "There was something in the paper today."

"And you want to talk about it." An enormous sigh escapes him, much as my last girl friend would sigh whenever I read something that disturbed me and wanted to talk. "Here he goes again," that sigh says. We only talked in bed.

But Dr. W is paid to listen. I get out the clipping:

"'Orange County's chief administrator plans to cut off payments for car repairs and bus fare to 3,400 general-relief recipients, a projected savings of $90 thousand.' $300 million in the hole, so they cut out bus fare, doesn't it make you sick?"

Dr. W's face shows not the slightest hint of expression or feeling.

"Don't you care, damn it! Those wonderful people denied an opportunity; the scoundrels at the top still with their six-figure salaries."

Dr. W's carefully manicured hands lay the clipping flat on his desk and begin to smooth out the creases. They are strong hands with long, tapered fingers, their nails cut short, fine dark hairs along the back of each one. When he speaks, finally, it is not what I want him to say.

"I care that you care. Help these people on welfare if you feel it will make good use of your time. Protest. Write a letter to the newspaper."

He looks off into the distance, strokes his forehead with the ends of his fingers before he turns back to me.

"Those wonderful stories about the homeless you've been writing: Pinkie and his friends. Why don't you try to sell them?"

I start to speak, contradict myself, babble, stop. Haven't I been here before half a dozen times with my own father? I think I could make money Dad, if I just sent away for... if I learned to play... if I asked her out. And always, instead of the magic I hope for, he would provide only steady, kind encouragement. Oh, why couldn't he have been a bastard.

"But what if my stories don't sell, what if nobody likes them?"

Like my father, Dr W's face remains placid, his manner imperturbable. Unlike my father, he cannot be made to feel guilty for his neglect of me.

"You've told me you've shown them to your friends and they like them."

"Friends. Who am I, Bette Middler?" I shake my head disparagingly, not sure why or what I stand for.

He looks me full in the face, his gaze unwavering, his steel-gray eyes making direct contact with mine for the first time since we began our sessions.

I flinch, look down at the thin tight knot of his plain red tie, pulled slightly to the left and below his collar button, the 100%-cotton oxford shirt blowing out and over his protruding paunch. I look past him to the bookshelves, at the framed diplomas, at everywhere but him.

I reach down. I touch the sadness.

www.ingramcontent.com/pod-product-compliance
Lightning Source LLC
LaVergne TN
LVHW090956080826
845145LV00003B/1023

* 9 7 8 0 9 8 4 1 6 0 3 6 5 *